INTRIGUE

Charlie Fox

CHAPTER ONE

A Body In The Woods

Finishing his final report relating to his most recent murder case, Detective Inspector Browne was thinking how different things looked from one season to another. When this case started the previous January, there had been a cold north wind blowing and the snow lay six inches deep across the mountain tops. When he started the investigation, he could never have imagined how complicated it would become. Getting caught up in another jurisdiction's diamond smuggling investigation, dealing with a group of ex- army comrades who shared a ten-year-old secret pledge of silence, a kidnapping on his doorstep, and a second murder all helped to make progress in the case very difficult. Today, with the investigation over, he was feeling relaxed, happily sitting drinking a glass of wine in his garden and enjoying the early Autumn sunshine. As he looked at the amount of documents he had to fill in, he thought how much easier it would be if there was just a little less paper work to be completed.

Every now and again his thoughts drifted from the case and focused on Elizabeth, his wife, who had gone into the city with Cathy, their eldest daughter, to look at wedding dresses. He was glad that he had not been asked to accompany them as, like most men, he did not like shopping. The wedding was still a year away but preparations had begun and many of the arrangements had already been finalised. Cathy, a school teacher in the local primary school, was marrying David, a dentist, who she had met while at college. If the engagement party was anything to go by, their wedding would be something very special. They were both lovers of music and could often be heard playing and singing in the local taverns. They were also keen athletes and every weekend enjoyed running cross country or cycling over high mountain trails. He was glad that he had started his 'Wedding Fund' many years earlier and found it hard to believe that his little girl had grown up so quickly and was now planning her wedding. It seemed only yesterday that he had been rocking her asleep in her cradle or holding her on his shoulders as they watched a parade pass by.

His thoughts were disturbed when the phone rang, and he was brought back to concentrating on his report by his DS reminding him of a meeting he was due to attend that evening. As he began to fill out the numerous forms, he thought back to that Monday morning when he had been advised by uniform that a body had been found in the woods about two miles outside the town.

With Detective Sergeant Jack Tobin by his side, he headed out to a carpark, nestled in the woods at the foot of the local mountains. It was a popular starting point for hill walkers with several sign-posted trails available to follow. The forest extended from the road right across the glen and almost to the top of the ridge five hundred metres above the fast-flowing river which passed through the glen below. The view from the ridge was stunning, especially when the sun highlighted the waterfall as it cascaded into the valley, and many hikers frequented the area daily taking photographs and making long lasting memories.

On arrival at the carpark, they were met by uniformed officers and escorted to the crime scene some half a mile inside the forest. The body of a lady was being examined by Dr Taylor and an officer was interviewing Patrick Jones, the man who had found the body. Mr Jones said that he had been out walking with his dog who had led him to the body with persistent barking. He had called the emergency services and waited for them to arrive. Mr Jones and his dog, Snap, lived only a short distance away and were daily walkers in the forest. Having given all the information that was required, man and dog set off home later than usual but with an unusual tale to tell. He had not told the Garda that he had seen Amelia, his wife, in the company of a man as she strolled through the forest, nor that he had a conversation with a friend only a few minutes before he found the body. He was aware of Amelia going out to the woods early each morning, collecting herbs and wild mushrooms, but he had never thought of her meeting anyone there. In the back of his mind he worried that they may have had something to do with the murder.

Dr Taylor, having completed a preliminary examination, told the inspector that the lady had died from a single blow to the back of her head and could have been there for forty-eight hours. He thought she was between thirty-five and forty and about five foot six inches in height. He said that he would have a more precise report after he performed the autopsy back at the morgue. At midday, the DI arranged for the removal of the body and organised an extensive search of the area, advising uniform to look carefully for anything that might help the investigation. Not finding a handbag, ID, or keys was unusual and he wondered if they had been taken by whoever had committed the crime. The woman was wearing black trousers, a white blouse with a short coat, and court shoes. She was certainly not dressed for hiking, nor for the freezing weather, and this led him to thinking about how she had arrived at that spot so far into the woods. Had she driven to the carpark? Had she been given a lift? If she had been brought in someone else's car would she have been forced to walk such a distance into the forest? Had she been out celebrating for the evening and come into the woods with a friend? Would she have been seen by anyone? If her bag and keys had been taken, would the assailant have driven off in her car?

There were four cars in the carpark. A red BMW standing alone, and three others each of whom were displaying mountain route cards indicating that the occupants were out hillwalking. The DI, not being an outdoor type, wondered why anybody would like to go walking in such cold, wintery conditions. He shivered at the thought of it and knew that he would be much happier returning to the Garda station and enjoying a nice cup of tea.

Efforts were being made to establish the identity of the car owners and it was quite possible that the BMW belonged to somebody out hillwalking. Until this was ascertained, an officer was posted with instructions to interview returning hikers and the car owners. DS Tobin, while checking the surrounding area, came across a large hollow with the remains of a fire in the centre. On closer inspection he observed that many people had been around the fire, and although the cold ashes indicated that it had not been used for some days he instructed the officers to include it in their search.

Patrick Jones, arriving home much later than usual, got a scolding from Amelia who had long-time doubts concerning his lone walks in the woods and often thought there could be another woman involved. When he finally got to speak about finding the body all she said was "I hope you had nothing to do with it." Patrick pointed out that she had also been out in the woods earlier collecting her mushrooms and wild herbs. He did not say that he had seen her as she strolled through the forest. He decided to be more vigilant on his walks and perhaps he could find out who it was that she was seeing. He would also need to ensure that she did not see him with his friend and knowing that she was already suspicious of him going out with Snap each morning he did wonder if she had been following him or indeed if she had seen him. She would never believe that they only met to exchange information on the badger population within the forest. They were both animal lovers and were doing a secret survey to ensure the safety of the badgers, whom they believed were under constant threat. Patrick, while out with Snap, kept a watch for snares or attempts to destroy their setts.

As soon as Amelia was alone she rang her friend Anthony and asked him if the Gardai had called to him. She told him about Patrick finding the body and he promised, if he was interviewed, not to mention their meeting in the forest earlier that morning. He knew that she had seen Patrick talking to a woman and wondered if this was the reason for her asking him not to mention their early morning meeting to the Gardai. Or was it that she worried that Patrick might get to know of their early morning get-togethers? Would she have thought it was that woman who had been murdered? Was she afraid that Patrick was the murderer? He realised that he would have to be careful what he said, if he was interviewed, as he knew in a murder investigation every word would be recorded and he could not afford to become a suspect.

CHAPTER TWO

Start Of The Investigation

Back in the Garda Station, an incident room was set up and all relevant information was channelled there. One piece of information on the notice board was the name and address of the owner of the red car found in the forest carpark. Her name was Meg Walsh and she lived at 22 Green Hill, an address on the outskirts of the town. An officer went to her house but as there was no sign of the occupants he thought that perhaps she had gone hillwalking and would turn up later in the day. He called to several nearby houses hoping to obtain some information on the residents. A close neighbour said that a young couple had moved into the house about a month earlier and although they had bid each other the time of day they had not had a conversation. She believed that they were in their late twenties, quite tall, and that the lady had long black hair and was always well dressed. While she had no further observations, her husband said that he thought he had seen a different lady coming and going but that it may have been the same lady his wife had seen. Other neighbours had only fleeting glances of the newcomers and could not describe them in any detail. Returning walkers, when being interviewed, confirmed that the red BMW was in the carpark when they started out at eight thirty that morning but they had not met anybody in the hills. As evening approached and no one had returned to the car it was removed to the station for safety and to undergo a forensic test if required.

Could the body in the morgue be Meg Walsh? Was the man seen with her involved? Was there a third person living in the house? How many hikers had ventured into the hills early that morning or on Sunday or even the day before on what was a really cold Saturday morning? Had anyone seen anything unusual as they walked through the forest? Would Patrick Jones have encountered anyone as he and Snap made their way through the woods? Who had left the fire remains in the hollow and had it any bearing on the case? These questions needed to be answered, so first thing on Tuesday morning the DI set out to speak with Patrick Jones while DS Tobin headed to the area around Green Hill.

First on his list was the hairdressing salon where he spoke to the owners, George Palmer and Pauline Smith. They had no recollection of anybody new having had their hair done during the previous week. Although a member of the local walking group, George had been walking alone on Sunday. However, as he had neither started nor finished in the car park, he had no knowledge concerning the cars that were parked there. He said that he had spoken to several walkers from the local walking group but had not seen any strangers. Pauline was not part of a walking group, as she preferred to tour on her motorbike at the weekends. She had not been out on Sunday as her bike was being repaired following a skid earlier in the week. She did not say that she had not been in the hills but as she had told the DS that she did not belong to a walking group, he never asked her.

The sports shop owner, John Oliver, had sold a pair of hiking boots to a new customer about two weeks earlier but had not seen her since. He had not noticed what cars were in the carpark on Sunday morning, perhaps because he was late arriving and was rushing to catch up with the rest of the group. From his receipt book, he identified the lady as Meg Walsh and offered her address to the DS. When other members of the walking group were being interviewed, Jack learned that John had been quite late that day, arriving very untidy and with traces of blood on his clothes. He had told them that while rushing to catch up, he had tripped on a tree root and had a nosebleed.

Another hiker was Anthony Gleeson, a café owner. He told the DS that he had not been out with the group on Sunday because his wife Betty, who usually ran the cafe on Sunday, was away with her friend Emily for a few days break so he was there instead. He explained that the group often met in the café to plan hikes and again after a walk to relax before going home. He did not recall seeing any unfamiliar faces in the café on Saturday or Sunday, except the walking group that arrived with June Thompson. He was busy at the time and did not pay particular attention to them. He was sure that June, the local mountain guide, would have all their details. After the DS left the café, Betty asked Anthony why he had said that she was away when he knew that she was out on the hills with her friend Emily. As he was not expecting this question, and not wanting Betty to find out about his meeting with Amelia, he had to think quickly and come up with a plausible answer. He could not tell her that he had been caught off guard when being interviewed and for a period had worried that they may have been involved in some way.

"Well" he said, " I knew that you were out on the hills with Emily but as she lives in the city I thought it would be better if we did not have to bring her back here to answer questions."

"What about yourself?" she replied. "You said nothing about going out early for your walk before coming back to open this place. I have nothing to hide! Do you?"

A customer entered at that moment, and Betty never got an answer. While she was attending to the customer, Anthony rang Amelia to confirm that he had a visit from the Gardai. He assured her that he had said nothing of their meeting. He knew that they would be getting together again soon and hoped they could continue to do so without Patrick or Betty finding out.

Dentist Sean Graham, another hike group member who had been in the hills with the group on Sunday, told the DS that he had looked after a young gentleman the previous week by the name of Jason O'Connor who lived at 22 Green Hill. His teeth had been fine. He had only asked to have them cleaned and he was looked after by the dental hygienist. Jason had told him that he had just moved into the area with his girlfriend, and had mischievously passed a remark that she would not be his girlfriend for much longer. This provided another name for the chart, and someone else to think about. As he was about to leave, a young lady came into the surgery and Sean introduced her as his girlfriend, June Thompson. June was a nurse in the local clinic, and a hill walker. As a qualified mountain guide she often took groups on local hikes as she had done, on Sunday, with a group of ten walkers. Remembering her name from an earlier interview, he spoke to her in relation to the visiting hikers. In an effort to eliminate this group, the DS got a list of everyone on the walk, the start and finish times, and the route followed. She told him that they had all stayed together for the duration of the walk and that everyone returned with her to the bus. He asked her to retain their addresses and phone numbers as he knew he may have to speak to them in the future. June did not recall anything unusual but promised to contact him if she did.

    His final call was to the newsagents where the owner, Declan O'Grady, spoke of a young couple who had been buying the evening paper for about three or four weeks but whom he had not seen since Wednesday. They were not always together, but one of them had enquired about having the papers delivered to their house. They had not made any definite arrangements so he did not have an address for them. His wife, Marge, said that the young lady was wearing an engagement ring and was always well dressed. When asked if he had been hiking on Sunday, Declan smiled and replied "no, Sargent, we both belong to the local hike group but Sunday is a busy day and we seldom get out with them at the weekends." After the DS left, Marge called Declan.
"You should have told him that you went out walking after we closed at six thirty." she said.
"Oh, I had forgotten about that!" he replied, "but as I was only out for a couple of hours and not with the group, he would hardly have been interested in that."
He had a strange feeling that she knew where he had been but found it hard to believe it to be possible. Marge, having followed him on a previous occasion, had her own ideas about where he had been but decided that it was not the best time to say anything. She had seen him meeting Mark, an unscrupulous former neighbour who she believed was involved with smuggling diamonds, and she feared that they were planning something underhand. She could not understand why, with the shop doing well, that he had to keep in touch with Mark and put himself in danger. Sometimes, she had a feeling that he

continued to miss the comradeship which he had shared many years before during his time in the army. She knew that Mark had never been in the army, but somehow, he seemed to be tied up with the comrades.

DI Browne, arriving at the Jones' house, was taken aback by Amelia Jones asking if her husband had been up to no good. "What has he been up to now? Always out in those woods, I never know what he is doing! Was he with another woman?" She continued rolling out some pastry with a formidable looking rolling pin as she called out to her husband that he had a visitor. Her exact words were "you're wanted." DI Browne discovered that Patrick Jones had seen several hikers making their way through the woods. Most of them he knew, as they belonged to the local hill-walking group. He did, however, remember speaking to a lady who asked him for directions to see the waterfall. Having received this information from him, she had continued on her way. The lady had told Patrick that she was aware of it being some distance away but she had been advised that she would have a clear view of it from that particular track. He remembered speaking to her because he had been conscious, at the time, of her not wearing clothes suitable for hillwalking or indeed for the wintery conditions. She was wearing a long dress, a light jacket, and court shoes, and he thought she was in her thirties or early forties. The DI wondered if it was just a coincidence to hear that neither this woman nor the victim were suitably dressed for the hills. Perhaps, he thought, they had started out together and their outing had ended in tragedy. Patrick said that he had not taken much notice of the carpark but thought there had been a few cars there. He said that his son Michael had also been in the hills that day but had returned to the city earlier that morning. Patrick did not mention that Michael was not with him but had been out (as Patrick thought), alone. The DI requested that he ask Michael to call to the station for a chat as soon as possible. The description of the lady that Mr Jones had given him did not match the corpse in the morgue and as it was he who had found the body he would have known if it was the same person. The DI felt it was important to locate this lady and eliminate her from the enquiries. He would have to find out if any of the hillwalkers had been talking to her.

CHAPTER THREE

Camping Overnight

Jason O'Connor and Meg Walsh had been hiking and camping in the woods the previous weekend, when they came across some unusual activity. As they prepared to go asleep on Saturday night, they heard voices coming from close by and, it being late, they stepped out of their tent and walked towards the sound. The area was lit up by a very bright full moon and flames from an open fire seemed to spiral up to meet the sky. There was a group of people around the fire and it was from here that the sound was coming. As they got closer to the site they saw what appeared to be a man with a goat's head leaning against a tall tree. Meg let out a cry, as most people would, which got the attention of the group. The goat-like man turned and walked away. The talking stopped and someone led them into the hollow. The short drop into the hollow seemed to take for ever and they were both very frightened. They heard one of the group say, "Who are you? What are you doing here? Are you reporters? What caused you to scream?" When Jason finally found his voice he explained that they were camping close by to continue their hike on Sunday morning. He told them that they were disturbed by the talking and as it was almost midnight decided to check out what was going on. A sigh of relief could be heard as Pat, the group leader, told then that they were a group of bird watchers having a cup of tea following the spotting of an unusual Owl which they heard had arrived the previous week. Jason and Meg stayed a while, chatting and enjoying a cup of tea, before heading back to their tent. They were a friendly bunch but knowing that people gathered in the hollow on the night of the full moon they were fearful that the location of the nest could have been discovered and the Owl harmed. Neither of them mentioned the eerie figure they had seen above the hollow.

Back in the tent Jason remained uneasy as he remembered that they had not seen the goat-like man after going into the hollow. Early next morning, as they were heading out on their hike, they noticed many footprints heading towards the carpark and another set going deeper into the forest. They wondered if they had anything to do with the strange sight they had witnessed or did they all belong to the group of bird watchers just going home in different directions. Following the picturesque trail they made their way towards the valley end where they would start climbing to the summit. Enjoying the scenery with the sound of the river flowing below them they soon forgot the events of the previous night as they concentrated on following their route card and compass bearings. Most of their conversation centred around their approaching wedding and honeymoon as they hoped that they had remembered and organised everything for their big day.

CHAPTER FOUR

Divorce Pending

On the Friday of the weekend that the body had been found, Lucy Delaney arrived to spend some time relaxing in the hills as she went through a difficult stage of her divorce. Only married for three years, it had been a trying period and her battle for freedom frustrating. She had met Bert, her husband, while they were serving in the Armed Forces. He was a sergeant in the army while she was serving in the army medical corps. He was a kind, loving person and she never expected, after only five months of marriage, to find him cheating on her. She could not bear to think of him with another woman and could certainly not go on living with him. He put all type of obstacles in her way and even threatened to kill any man he thought she was seeing. This made her more determined than ever to get a divorce and to meet as many men as possible. Her lifestyle changed drastically as she went from one lover to another and realised how boring life had been with him. Seeing the way she was carrying on, Bert became very angry and swore that he would put a stop to it as soon as he could organise some leave.

Lucy, a seasoned hillwalker with thoughts of spending some time hiking, had taken a train to a town close to the mountains and checked into a small hotel. She booked a meal with plans of having an early night. The restaurant atmosphere was very pleasant with soft background music and an efficient waiter service. There was an interesting menu and the meal was served promptly. The accompanying wine was perfect with her beef fillet and following a few glasses of Cotes de Rhone, thoughts of an early night were forgotten and she made her way across the road to the night club in the casino. The bar was quite lively with a group playing eighties music which was greatly appreciated by those on the dance floor.

It was not long after she had ordered a drink that she was asked if she would like to dance. He was tall and good-looking with a boyish grin and she was thrilled to get a chance of enjoying a relaxing time with somebody new. Leaving her glass on the table she stood up and took to the floor, a little surprised at the attention she was getting from around the hall. Being from the city she was not aware of how a stranger stood out in a small town where all the locals knew each other. Had she been more observant she would have seen a number of very jealous local girls. The music was enchanting and she floated around the floor holding a conversation with this complete stranger as if she had known him all her life. The topics were many and varied and she was very much at ease as they danced to the sound of the eighties. At the end of what seemed like a long time the band stopped playing and she reluctantly went back to her drink. She was not alone for long. She had only started to drink her Bacardi when she was once again on her feet, her admirer not giving anyone else a chance to ask her to dance. They enjoyed each other's company and spent the rest of the evening dancing or sitting together. As they both loved hiking and he knew the local area they arranged to meet on Sunday morning and spend a few hours together in the hills. His name was Michael Jones and he stayed with his parents Patrick and Amelia at the weekends. They lived in the family home which was close to the forest car park. Telling her that he would pick her up at the hotel at eight thirty on Sunday morning he headed home. She could not believe her luck as she considered how fortunate she had been not only to have met Michael but that he was also a hillwalker and they could enjoy walking in the mountains together. She hoped that she could relax for the couple of weeks and face the daunting divorce proceedings when she returned home.

CHAPTER FIVE

The Casino

On Thursday morning DS Tobin, on arrival at the station, was advised by the duty officer that a young lady was waiting in his office wishing to speak to him. Charlotte Robinson explained that she was a member of a bird watchers' group who met weekly in the local bar and when she read of the murder and the car being found in the forest carpark she felt that she should tell of the night in the forest. As it had taken place the previous weekend she was not sure that it was connected but something that she thought odd on the night might be of interest. Her group had been out trying to spot a rare Owl which had been reported to them the previous week. They were having a cup of tea, in a hollow which they often used to have a break while out at night, when a couple appeared above them and the lady let out a terrific scream. They were brought down as they both looked very frightened and we wondered who they were ad why they were in the forest so late at night. They said that they were camping and had come over when they heard our voices. Afterwards, Charlotte remembered that they had never mentioned the cause of the scream.

She told the DS of another reason for them being in the woods that night. It was the night of the full moon and they had heard that a ritual was being held there and hoped by their presence they would prevent the participants from learning of the Owl's location. When asked if she knew any of the people involved with the ritual, she hesitated before answering a definite no. There had been talk of a coven of friendly witches but she had always believed it to be a joke. She thought they met in a casino about five miles away but was unsure of its exact location. As this had happened a week prior to the murder and nothing had been found around the hollow during the search, the DS decided that it did not tie in with the murder. He got her phone number and asked her for a list of those who were there on the night with her. Escorting her to the door he could not describe the warm feeling he experienced but he knew that he would have to meet her again very soon. She was the most beautiful girl he had ever seen and he could not get her out of his thoughts. Concentrating on the case became almost impossible as the vision of her filled his mind. No other girl had ever affected him like this and he certainly had never expected anything like that to happen while on duty. He was so happy that he had secured her phone number even if it had been officially. He thought that he should have asked her out while he had the chance and knew that he would do so at the first possible opportunity.

Thinking that the casino might yield some information he decided to pay it a visit. As it was outside his jurisdiction he went to the superintendent for permission. He was surprised to be refused and when he tried to explain he was told that until it was established that the car or the unidentified corpse were connected to the casino he was required elsewhere. He really felt that the casino could reveal something new so he decided to seek the help of his friend William. Detective William Byrne and Jack had joined the force together and had remained good friends ever since. William who was stationed near the casino listened to his friend and promised to discreetly investigate the activities there. Several facts were revealed during his surveillance. Charlotte Robinson had attended meetings there even though she had said that she did not know where it was. John Oliver, the sports shop owner, was also seen there as was Leo Fitzgerald a close friend of superintendent Daly. As well as being a casino it housed a bar, a dance hall and private rooms where meetings were held so there were always people coming and going. William had a few friends who frequented the bar and he obtained some informal information from them. They told him that the bar could be described as a good place to socialise and would be a starting point for disco goers or those going to have a flutter in the casino. It had a good reputation and seemed to cater for a mixed clientele. One thing that struck William was the number of meetings held in a private room over the bar which was restricted to members only. No one had any knowledge of the group or how you could join. Someone had jokingly said that they might be witches but not much heed was given to that by anyone. At some point in time memories of what had said concerning witches came to mind and gave him food for thought. He had planned on ringing Charlotte, as her image was constantly on his mind, but now knowing that she had denied any knowledge of the casino but had been seen there on a couple of occasions he decided to hold back. He could not believe that such a beautiful girl would have had anything to do with a murder and he was very tempted to ring her. His training and common sense dictated that he do the right thing and with reluctance he decided to wait and see how things worked out. The following morning, having completed the post mortem, Dr Taylor advised Inspector Brown of his findings. The lady, he thought, was between twenty-five and thirty-five and was five foot six inches in height. One item that had puzzled him was a coating of purple colouring on her face but he thought that it could have been some form of makeup which he would have analysed. She had died from a single blow with a blunt instrument to the back of her head or a karate chop which would have had the same effect. There were no signs of a struggle so he concluded that she had been taken by surprise or knew her killer. He believed that her attacker must have been strong to inflict such a wound with one blow. There were no traces of bark or soil at the wound site so he felt a hammer handle or something similar had been used. Had she been out with a friend and had a row leading to her death? Was she just attacked for her hand bag and car keys? Was it a robbery gone terribly wrong? An extensive search for the murder weapon had been made but nothing had been found. The incident room information board was filling up with names, photos, suggestions and current ideas trying to link all of the aspects together. Not knowing the identity of the corpse and not having a murder weapon made putting things in place exceedingly difficult. There were no reports of a missing person so it was believed that the lady could have been on holidays and had not yet been missed by her family. Thoughts of who might be involved were being discussed by the team when superintendent Daly came in to assess the situation. Following her inspection she asked the DI to join her in her office. DS Tobin wondered what was going on and as he was part of the investigation felt that if there was a problem he should know about it. On his return the DI advised Jack that the casino was off limits unless specific instructions were given by the superintendent. There was no explanation but Jack knew he would have to abide by it. As soon as he got a chance he rang his friend William and told him to stay clear of the casino in case there was an investigation going on that he was not privy to. William, like Jack, wondered about this but promised he would stay away until things got a little clearer.

On Saturday, while looking through his notes, DI Browne realised that John Oliver, the owner of the sports shop, had met Meg Walsh when she bought a pair of walking boots and wondered if he could identify the body in the morgue. When asked John suggested ringing Meg Walsh first hoping he would not have to go to the morgue at all. Not getting a reply he reluctantly agreed to accompany the two officers to where the body was being kept. He did not like the idea of seeing someone in that environment especially when it could be a person that he might recognise. He went in bravely and was pleased when he could not identify her. He said that he did not remember seeing anyone dressed like that around the town. He was asked not to reveal anything about her attire as this may be crucial at a later stage.

As they were leaving the DI got a call from the super telling him to contact her when he returned to the station. He soon learned that a handbag had been found in the bar at the casino and it may be connected to the present case. He went over to collect it immediately and learned that Denis Barker, the barman, had found it under a chair on Monday morning but held on to it thinking the owner would return looking for it. When asked if he remembered who was sitting in that place he explained that he had a day off on Sunday and had not been there. Looking at the contents back at the incident room they were surprised not to find any cash, keys or ID. Various other items were found which for security reasons were not divulged. It seemed strange that a handbag which was obviously brought for a night out had none of these things present. Was it in any way related to the murder? Had the murderer taken everything and if so why? Was it that the bag had been stolen, emptied, and left in the bar? Perhaps it was just a case of the owner, having had a few drinks, going home without it. She may not have remembered where she had left it but if this was the case it was strange that there were no keys or cash in it. Had the bar staff anything to do with it? Knowing that the barman was off on Sunday and could possibly have been in the woods he added him to the list for further questioning.

CHAPTER SIX

Jason and Meg Getting Married

Jason O'Connor and Meg Walsh drove to the city, on the Thursday prior to the murder, to get married. It was a low-key affair as they had preferred to put their money into buying their new house and on an expensive elongated honeymoon. Eva Armstrong, their bridesmaid, went with them and following the wedding and family reception drove them to the airport from where they flew on their long awaited around the world tour. Mags drove the car back to their house and parked it in the driveway. She had made plans to visit a friend in Australia while the couple were away and went to the station and boarded a train at nine twenty-five to return to her house in the city. Falling asleep as the train sped along the tracks she did not notice her handbag being removed and later being put back beside her. On arriving home she realised that Meg's car keys were missing and rang the train company to see if they had been found on the train. She was sure she had put them in her bag and could not understand how they had disappeared. She tried to recall the train journey but as she had been asleep for some of it had only vague memories. She did remember her ticket being checked and the buffet attendant having a conversation with a tall man who got off the train before the final stop. She had not taken notice of anyone else. It worried her that someone might find the keys and use them to steal the car until she realised that there was no identification on them. She would have to let Meg know but as she did not wish to tell her while she was on honeymoon she decided to send her a letter which she would get when she returned. She never thought of advising the Gardai who, had they known, could have kept the car under observation.

CHAPTER SEVEN

Unanswered Questions

On Sunday morning there were more and more questions and not being able to speak to Meg Walsh nor Jason O'Connor was proving difficult and brought all type of thoughts into the equation. Could there be more bodies in the forest? What instrument was used to murder the lady? DS Tobin had his own ideas as he studied the ever-increasing information on the notice board. Was there a connection between the casino and the enquiry? Was it possible that a coven of witches did exist? Did they have any bearing on the case? Was the superintendent hiding something? Why would her friend Leo Fitzgerald frequent the casino so regularly? Was he working for the super? Should he interview Charlotte Robinson again? Since meeting her he could not get the vision of her out of his head and wondered if he could talk to her without letting his feelings show. His main worry was that she had denied knowing where the casino was situated yet had been seen going there. He felt a huge urge to see her and hoped that she had no knowledge of the murder. He became totally consumed with thoughts of her and found it difficult to concentrate on his job.

The DI and Jack tried to tie in the pieces of information but they just seemed fragmented and did not lead anywhere. "Should we search the woods again? Are there more bodies to be found? Would it help if we interviewed all those that were out on the hills that weekend again? Should we get uniform to go from house to house and see if anybody, yet unknown, had been in the hills on either Saturday or Sunday? If we could just interview Jason and Meg and hear what they had to say? Did they have anything to do with the murder or were they victims also? Should we seek permission to check the casino?" Jack could not help feeling that they were missing something and wondered what it might be that had escaped them. The DI took the decision to have the woods searched again, interview all those that had been out walking and speak to all the bird watchers who, he knew, had been in the hollow the previous weekend. He sent his sergeant to speak with the bird watchers and said that he would interview the hikers himself. While thinking about the interviews he wondered if Jason and Meg had gone on holidays. He asked uniform to check flight logs and ferry passenger lists but neither enquiry showed any results. It was not known that they had booked their flights long before their wedding with Meg travelling on her passport name of Margaret Walsh and Jason with his proper name of Jayceon O' Connor, both with address in the city, and so were not connected to the names and address given by the Gardai.

During the week, prior to the murder, Jim, one of Luke's charity group who met behind closed doors in the casino, had been looking for a getaway car which he would need to have in readiness very soon. Seeing a red BMW passing through the town a few times he thought that it would be suitable so followed it to its destination and watched it being parked. He continued watching the house during the week and observed the couple arriving home at the same time each evening. On Thursday he waited to see it being parked in its usual place and could not believe it when it did not turn up on time. He waited patiently for an hour and was rewarded as it drove into the driveway. It was driven by a different lady who did not go into the house but walked towards the town centre. Leaving his own car he followed her hoping to get a chance, in a bar or restaurant, to grab her bag and remove the car keys. He was surprised when she went to the station and boarded a train for the city. He bought a ticket and followed her on board. Sitting a few seats behind her he watched as she fell asleep. He could not believe his luck as he lifted her bag, removed the keys and replaced the bag on her seat. Before getting off the train he had a cup of tea and a conversation with the catering attendant. After getting off the train he rang a friend and arranged a lift back to his car. He watched the house on Friday and Saturday and not seeing anyone coming or going he decided that he would take the car on Sunday and keep it hidden until it was needed.

CHAPTER EIGHT

Making A Date

Jack, on seeing Charlotte as part of his bird watchers' interviews, was spellbound and could not ignore her magnetic attraction. They sat in the winter sun enjoying a coffee talking and laughing as if there was not a problem in the world. She watched him carefully as she wondered if this had to do with the murder or was it a more personal meeting. She hoped it was that he liked her as she felt drawn to him from the moment they met in the Garda station. He had planned to ask her about her visits to the casino but could not bring himself to do so. Eventually he had to tell her that he was looking for information and they went through everything just like before. Nothing had changed and her account of the night was exactly as she had reported it. She said that she had only a few minutes conversation with the couple that night and only repeated what he had already heard. The atmosphere was a little cooler but he was sitting beside the most beautiful girl he had ever seen and really wanted to ask her out. He knew that he should wait until the investigation was completed but she had taken over his thoughts since they last met and seeing those beautiful brown eyes and her open smile his heart took over and he blurted out an invitation. She was not sure who was asking her out; was it the detective or the man. Did he feel as she did? Was his heart racing as fast as hers? Why now she thought, I am in about the most dangerous position of my life and cannot afford this distraction but as she was also feeling a huge attraction agreed to meet on Monday evening. They arranged time and place and parted both hoping they had done the right thing.

Charlotte, being the youngest of four children, had up to now concentrated on her career and had not been bothered socialising. At college she had dated a couple of lads but never long enough to get serious. Most of her friends were engaged or had steady boyfriends but this had never deterred her from trying to achieve her ambition. Suddenly meeting Jack changed everything and she started dreaming of what might lie ahead.

As Jack headed towards the incident room he had mixed feelings and felt very uneasy. He knew he should have spoken to her about the casino and hoped it would not interfere with the investigation. He soon had himself convinced that such a beautiful girl could not have had anything to do with the murder and relaxed. As he passed the local bar he saw Sean Graham the dentist going in with John Oliver but as it was lunch time he put it out of his thoughts.

DI Browne, working through his list of hikers, noticed that two of the group that had been out hiking with June Thompson had not been in touch with him. Joan Davis and Angela Winters had the same address in the city so he attempted to contact them by phone. There was no answer and although he left messages they never responded. He decided to ask the officers in their area to make contact with them. That evening he received a call advising him that neither of the ladies were at home and nobody knew where they might be. The officers would continue to look for them and would get back in touch as soon as possible. In the meantime he had called to speak to June Thompson and had asked her if she had any knowledge of the ladies. She only knew that somebody had recommended her to them and they had contacted her by phone. It was the same number that she had given to the DS on her list of hikers for that day. She did not remember much about them except that they had not mixed with anyone else and left quickly and quietly following the hike. That was not unusual following a walk as many of the walkers would have a bus or a train to catch. She could not say if they had a car as they had all met in the café and were transported, by mini coach, to and from the carpark in the forest. There had been ten adults in the group and all of them had stayed together for the few hours. She did not think that any of them had strayed far and they had only stopped to admire the scenery or to take photographs. Some of them had spent some time in the café before dispersing. He advised June that he would have to speak to each of them and would need a longer conversation with her. She had also been in the café having a coffee but could not remember how many of the group had been there. The café owner, Anthony Gleeson, had no idea either but looked up the visitor's book to see if they had left any comments. None were found and on that day only a few customers had signed it.

DS Tobin returned to the forest as requested by the DI and heard voices while walking close to where the body had been found. He was surprised to see Patrick Jones, with his arm around a young woman, as he walked with Snap along the forest track. Holding back he watched as they talked and laughed until they reached a turn in the path. Thoughts of his wife's words "was he with another woman" came back to him and he wondered about the corpse in the morgue. After a short conversation they split up and went their separate ways leaving Jack to wonder if this turn of events would have any bearing on the case. He followed her until she came to a clearing where a young man was sitting on a motorbike waiting for her. She lost no time getting on the bike and they drove off without seeing him. He made a note of the registration so that he could check it back at the station. He continued to look around the site but found nothing new.

His mind was more on Charlotte than on his work as he thought of meeting her again and he was finding concentrating on the case very difficult. He was light hearted as he walked back to his car and so happy that they had met. He could not believe that his life had changed so suddenly from mundane to exceptional just by meeting Charlotte. He wanted to sing and tell the world of his new found happiness as visions of her beauty flashed across his mind. He was totally preoccupied with the thoughts of their date and could not think of anything else.

Arriving back at the forest carpark he was taken completely by surprise when he saw the motorbike parked there but no sign of anyone. His concentrating levels suddenly took an upward surge as he thought about the couple. He asked himself why would they have waited, in the middle of the forest, to meet Patrick and then drive to the carpark? Where had they gone to? Was she in any danger? He decided to ring base and find out to whom the bike was registered. In a matter of minutes he learned that it belonged to Pauline Smith with an address in the town and he now understood why the girl had looked familiar even at a distance. The address was the hairdressing saloon and he could only smile as he made his way in that direction. He wondered what, if any, was the relationship between George Palmer and Pauline. Would he know that she was seeing Mr Jones? Did they both live at the saloon or was it just a convenient address to register the bike? At the salon George confirmed that Pauline had a motorbike and on her day off usually went out into the country for a ride. George said that she lived over the saloon with her husband and that he had an apartment not far away in the town. He was married with two children and work was their only connection. He told Jack that she had been living there since she got married about six months earlier. Jack wondered was the man on the bike her husband and what was the connection with Patrick Jones. He, knew that he, would have to follow this up very quickly.

CHAPTER NINE

Meeting At The Casino

On Monday morning, one week before the murder, the private room over the Casino was occupied, a meeting was taking place that not even the owner knew what it was about. There had been a rumour, in the bar, that it could have been a coven of witches and as it seemed to intrigue his clients he never denied it. Had he known what was going on there he may have had cause to worry. In the room were four men, Luke their leader, Gareth, Mark and Jim along with four ladies Margaret, Mary, Tina and Charlotte counting large sums of cash and carefully placing it into a briefcase. Without a word Luke and Margaret left with the cash and drove away in a stylish car. The remaining group sat around a large table discussing collections, deliveries and meeting points during which time names and possible locations were decided upon. On their return Luke and Margaret, now without their briefcases, joined in the discussions. There were still a few weeks before the journey to Holland but they began making arrangements for Gareth to fly to Amsterdam with the cash and hand it over to their charity collection counterparts. Luke said that his yacht would be ready to sail if needed and Jim assured them that he would have a car organised before then. As they left the room and made their way down the stairs they encountered Dr Taylor on his way to the restaurant. Charlotte greeted him and had a few words as they continued on their way out. The Doc, aware of the rumours concerning witches, laughed to himself as he tried to picture her on a broomstick. He did wonder what type of meeting she had been attending but put it down to another hike related group. Mark asked who it was she had been speaking to and could it cause any problems. Answering she told him that if anyone asked about the meeting she would say that they had been discussing the Owl sightings and not mention the charity. That explanation seemed all right and the subject was dropped. She did wonder how her conversation could cause a problem.

She was thinking about her date with Jack later that evening and hoped that she was doing the right thing. She would have to remember not to mention the Casino and hoped if Dr Taylor was speaking to Jack he would not mention having met her there. She was due to meet Gareth in the afternoon and give him the tickets for his trip in three weeks' time to Amsterdam. Just before two thirty as she made her way to the meeting with Gareth she began to feel uneasy and thought that she was being followed. Making a detour she went into the bar and out the side door where she saw Mark, the one who had quizzed her about speaking to the doc, trying to work out where she had gone. This worried her and for some strange reason she felt in danger. She rang Gareth and arranged a different meeting place. She went back home, got her car, and set out for the new meeting point. Gareth met her and said that Mark had rung him asking why she had not delivered the flight tickets at the crossroads as planned. He believed that Mark was annoyed but did not know why. Answering him she said, "he knew the plan so why follow me? Why take this action on his own? He was aware that the only reason for me getting the tickets, from my friend who works in the travel agency, was that she appreciated that we were doing charitable work and gave me a discount." Gareth said that he was also confused with his action, "perhaps he thought that we had something going on and were planning to go off together. He knew why we were meeting and had no reason to mistrust us. Oh Charlotte, I really do not know what way he thinks at times maybe he thought that he should be going to Amsterdam not me. Just forget all about it, once we get through these next few weeks we can settle down and relax before starting our next charity drive." Charlotte tried to understand Mark's intrusion but could not find an answer. Had he some personal reason for not trusting her or was it Gareth he was having problems with? One way or the other she could not understand why there should be any confusion over handing over a couple of travel tickets.

CHAPTER TEN

Jack And Charlotte's Secret Meeting

Meeting Jack that evening Charlotte soon forgot all her worries as they relaxed together having a meal and a few drinks in the local bar. The conversation was easy and fluid and the magic they both felt brought them ever closer. On arrival at her apartment Charlotte invited him in for a coffee and they spent the rest of the night together. It was a truly magical night during which they were both convinced that they were physically as well as mentally suited. It was a beautiful feeling waking up in the morning knowing your instinct was correct. Falling in love so quickly had not been on the cards for either Charlotte nor Jack but it had happened and there was not a lot they could do about it. They were so wrapped up in each other that consequences were not considered. They were both still feeling the joy of their night together and wished that they did not have to go to work. They reluctantly parted with thoughts of seeing each other soon again. Still in a dream world they went their separate ways and neither of them could get the beautiful feelings, they were experiencing, out of their system.

Arriving at the station, on that Tuesday morning, Jack was abruptly brought down to earth as he and the DI were called into the superintendent's office. The atmosphere was tense and Jack knew that something must have gone terribly wrong but had not thought, for a moment, that it had anything to do with him. The super came straight to the point and Jack heard her say "Last evening Jack you were in the company of a young lady who, as you are aware, might be involved in our murder enquiries. This is not a desirable position and I have no option but to advise you to stop seeing her immediately." Jack's heart missed a beat and he could not find the words to say that made any sense. His first reaction was to protect this beautiful girl, his beautiful girl, but off course he knew that it would be of no help. He agreed not to see her again but in his heart he knew that he would. Then something was said that turned his thinking on its head. The super instructed the DI to have her picked up for questioning and to ensure that DS Tobin did not have an opportunity of speaking to her. She then advised Jack to remain in the station until such time as she was brought in and told him to leave his mobile in her care. Another turn of events unfolded and compounded an already unsettling situation. A report from uniform division, who were trying to build up information on the time around the murder, focused on a report by the train company of a lady who had reported losing car keys a few days before the murder. The main interest was that the address given was the same as Meg Walsh's. There was no name or phone number on record which was strange as the clerk, who took the call, remembered getting a number which he had used to advise the lady that the keys had not been found on the train.

The DI asked uniform to interview those working on the station or on the train that Thursday night. It emerged that the train had departed at nine-thirty with twenty passengers on board. The inspector and the driver, being interviewed, told of an uneventful journey but Colm O Hara the snack bar attendant could not be interviewed as he was away, on a few weeks leave, visiting his daughter in New Zealand. He had been working on the trains for about a year since retiring from the army and he was spoken very highly of by anyone who knew him. He was left a message to contact the DI on his return. The inspector remembered one lady who was asleep soon after leaving and knew he had seen her ticket later but could not recall where she was going to. He was able to give the names of six passengers as they lived locally and he knew them all well. As far as he could remember there were two ladies with rucksacks, a group of about five tourists, French he thought, two elderly couples, a lady who said that she had been hiking all day and a tall man who spent some time speaking to the snack bar attendant. This had all happened a few days before the murder but the DI could not help thinking that the missing keys could be connected in some way.

Charlotte was apprehended and brought to the Garda station. Escorted by a Garda she was taken to Superintendent Daly in the interview room. She protested and made it quite clear that she was extremely annoyed at this turn of events and said her solicitor would sort it out very quickly. She asked why would they need to speak to her about a murder since she was nowhere near the woods that weekend. The superintendent advised her that her being brought to the station was about her visits to the casino, in particular her attending meetings behind closed doors. Charlotte heard her say, "What exactly are these meetings about, we know you belong to a bird watchers' group and are a hill walker but none of the other members of these groups frequent the casino. Up until now, as it is outside of our jurisdiction, we never took any interest in the casino but this is a murder enquiry and you denied any knowledge of it when speaking to DS Tobin and yet the next day you were seen going to a meeting there. Perhaps you would like to explain that to me." Charlotte was agitated and for a while refused to say a word. When she did speak, it was in a low controlled voice as she told the superintendent that she also belonged to an anonymous fund-raising group who collected and distributed funds to deserving causes. "We meet in this manner as it serves our purpose and gives us the opportunity to achieve privacy without, up to now, anybody taking any notice of us. I really hope that this goes no further as we would find it difficult to get another convenient meeting place." Knowing that the group was under surveillance, by the international Garda division, the superintendent had to be incredibly careful as she did not wish to interfere with, what might be, a serious investigation. She did not fully believe Charlotte's story but decided that the best thing to do was to step aside and see how things worked out. Advising Charlotte, that for the moment, no further action would be taken but said that she did not know what may be required in the future.

Charlotte left the station a little shocked at the prospect of the super doing a follow up. Would she find the truth about the group and more worrying for her was the thoughts of the grilling she would get if any of the group had seen her being taken to the station. Her main fear was soon realised as Luke, the group leader, stopped her and invited her to have a coffee in the café. She knew immediately that he had seen her being brought to the Garda station and wanted to know how high the risk of them being discovered was. She began to formulate the answers that she might need and hoped that he would believe her. He was quite aggressive and she found it all very intimidating. He went to great lengths to remind her of the level of security necessary especially during these last-minute negotiations with their charity partners in Amsterdam. She explained that, as far as she was concerned, the superintendent had accepted the necessity for privacy when doing this type of charity work. She felt that he did not believe her but he just said that they would have to wait and see what transpired. Leaving the café she knew things were changing and she would have to be more careful in the future. She was surprised as she left to see Luke in deep conversation with Anthony Gleeson the café owner and wondered if he was involved in some way with Luke.

CHAPTER ELEVEN
Michael Jones Hillwalking

True to his word, on Sunday morning, Michael Jones arrived at the hotel to meet up with his date from Friday night at the casino. They drove to the carpark and set out for a day's hiking. Heading up towards the distant peaks their conversation, like the previous evening at the dance, was easy and free flowing and they both felt that they may not spend the full day walking. Stopping for lunch in the shelter of a peat hag, even though the day was cold, they fell into each other's arms and wondered why their last encounter had not ended up the same way. Coffee and sandwiches abandoned they lustfully explored each other and with gay abandon let nature take its course. It was as if time stood still and the thrill of being together brought them to greater heights than either had ever experienced and they were reluctant to let it end. Finally the weather, which was now cold and wet, decided it for them and they returned to the car already looking forward to their next meeting. It may have been a different story had they realised that they had been followed earlier from the hotel and observed all day. Michael, promising to see her again the following week, left her at the hotel and headed home.

She booked a table for the evening meal, got a drink at the bar and went to her room to have a shower. Clutching the glass of Cote de Rhone she opened the door and made her way inside. Feeling elated following her earlier lovemaking she slipped out of her clothes and still holding her glass of wine stepped into the shower. She experienced a warm sensual feeling as the scented water caressed her soft pale skin. She remained under the flowing water thinking back on her afternoon of sheer delight and dreaming of their next encounter. Dressed and ready to go down for dinner, Lucy was surprised to hear a knock on her door. Opening it she was confronted by a waiter who explained that he had been instructed to accompany her to the restaurant. Checking that she had her cash and keys in her handbag she headed down with him. As they passed a side door he bundled her out and straight into a waiting car which sped away at great speed. As they drove away the driver said something to the lady beside him and she in turn asked the man sitting in the back to give her Lucy's handbag. As her would be waiter did this he said that they were taking her to a friend and that was the only conversation for the whole journey. Two hours later they stopped at an isolated country cottage and her worst fears were realised as she saw her husband waiting for her and heard him casually inviting her in. Once she was inside he ordered the others to leave and told her to make herself comfortable. He had a meal prepared but she was in no humour of eating. "What is this all about" she asked him as he continued to eat his meal. "You will not get away with this I will be missed very soon and they will be looking for me." "Who exactly will miss you" he answered. "If somebody does where will they start looking. Nobody would think of you going so far in a couple of hours. You are going to stay here and think about our future together. Spending some time alone here you will realise that there is no reason for a divorce." Taking her mobile out of her bag he said, "you will not need this" and handing her back her handbag told her to go into the sitting room and make herself comfortable. "The house is locked and alarmed so trying to get out before I return would be a waste of time. You can spend the next few days thinking of our pending divorce and see if you can come up with a better solution." With that he went out and she heard him drive away. She was tempted to break out but was afraid that he may have returned and was waiting, in the car, to hear the alarm going off. Realising it was late and dark she decided to go to bed and think what she would do in the morning. Waking up, after a restless night, it was obvious that she was in the middle of nowhere and had no idea where she was. She was sure that he would return in a few days and started to formulate a plan of action. She felt that if she had any hope of getting out of this situation she would have to convince him that she had changed her mind and would work with him to sort it all out. Not knowing exactly how he was thinking she hoped he would agree to take her to the hotel so that she could collect all her belongings before making their way home. Once she got to the hotel she knew that she could get help and escape from him. If she was lucky she might even be able to get him arrested and charged with kidnapping her. She knew that she would never live with him again and hoped he would be arrested before he had time to do anything rash. That the Gardai would not believe her story never crossed her mind and she looked forward to being free again soon. She checked the windows and doors but could not find any easy way out of the house. She hoped it would not take him too long to return.

CHAPTER TWELVE

Jim In The Carpark

Jim, who had stolen the car on Sunday morning and hid it in his garage, had not expected to need it for a couple of weeks but an ex-army comrade needed a favour. It was a straight forward job, pick up a lady at her apartment and another lady at the hotel and bring them to a cottage some two hours' drive away. He was surprised when he also picked up a waiter at the apartment. On arrival at the hotel the waiter instructed him to drive to the side door and wait for him there. He did not know what to expect but up until now things had turned out differently than he had imagined. Moments later the waiter bundled a lady into the back seat and ordered him to drive away quickly. Other than giving him directions, as he drove, not another word was spoken. It took two hours to reach their destination where the waiter escorted the lady into the cottage. He came straight back out and taking another two hours they arrived back at the apartment where he left them. Worrying that the car may have been picked up by a security camera he decided he would need a different one for the original job for which he had taken it. He could not leave it back so decided to drive it to the forest carpark and leave it there. It was then about two o'clock, dark and cold so as he was very tired he decided to sleep in the car for a few hours. Later as he walked down towards the road he heard voices and hid behind some bushes until they went by.

Giving them a few minutes he started off again but tripped on a tree root and fell over. He never noticed the car keys falling out of his pocket as he picked himself up and headed home. As he walked along the dark road he wondered why the two people were heading into the woods at that hour on a Monday morning.

CHAPTER THIRTEEN

Missed Meal Booking

At half past eight, as Lucy had not arrived at the restaurant, the head waiter phoned her room but got no reply. He enquired at the reception desk but nobody had seen her leave. Thinking she had fallen asleep he sent a waiter to her room to call her. She was not there but as all her belongings were they assumed that she had forgotten about the booking and had gone out for the night. On Monday, Nathan Clarke, the hotel manager rang the Gardai alerting them to the possibility of a missing lady. The DS called over to interview the staff and check her room. He instructed the manager to lock the room until a forensic team arrived and he informed the DI. Inspector Browne agreed with him and came over to check the room himself. The forensic team, except for staff, found only one set of unidentified fingerprints so it was believed that they belonged to Lucy Delaney. There was no sign of a struggle or of anybody else having been in the room. One interesting item found was a return train ticket from the city which indicated that she intended staying in the area for two weeks. In the safe they saw legal papers showing that she was going through divorce proceedings. These confirmed her name and gave her husband's name and address offering them a new line of enquiry. Was she the murder victim? Was he connected in any way? Did he have reason to see his wife murdered? Would they now find parents and siblings? Had she told anybody that she was going away? Would anybody look for her knowing that she had gone away for two weeks? None of the staff had seen anybody else in the room but a resident said that she saw a man going out the side door carrying a suitcase but as this was quite usual in a hotel she thought no more about it. The hotel CCTV did not cover the side entrance that night, as the camera was being repaired, but the front of house camera showed Lucy being dropped off by Michael Jones who then drove off in the direction of his home. No other sighting of her was seen that evening and had she been going across the road to the casino she would have used the main door. A man was seen lurking around the hotel shortly after Lucy arrived but he did not seem to enter the building. Could he have gone around to the side door and if he had would that indicate that he was familial with the hotel. Watching the front of house CCTV tapes was tiresome until a car was seen pulling into the lane where the side entrance of the hotel was situated. The main interest was that it was a red BMW and although the number plate could not be seen both the DI and DS were convinced that it was the one found in the forest car park. Could this be the reason that Lucy had not been seen leaving? Had she simply slipped out the side door into a waiting car? Had she been carried out in a suitcase? This put a different slant on the car which up to now had been just considered a lost vehicle. It was handed over to forensics for a complete check. As keys for the car had not been found the speciality group, under the supervision of the DI, obtained a duplicate set from the makers and set about their examination. No traces of anything unusual were found in the car even after extensive testing. Many fingerprints were found but none showed up on their computer. There were none on the steering wheel so it was believed that the driver had worn gloves or had wiped it clean before abandoning it.

CHAPTER FOURTEEN
Bert Delaney Located

Having the name and address of Lucy's husband, the DI contacted the local Gardai and asked them to get Bert Delaney to get in touch. He got a call within the hour and was surprised when Bert agreed to come down immediately and see if he could identify the body. The DI explained that it may not be his wife but as the body had been found nearby and his wife was missing locally he would like to eliminate her from his enquiries if possible. On arrival Bert, in full army uniform, marched quickly into the morgue leaving his accompanying Garda rushing in behind him. One quick look and he turned to the DI and without emotion said, "no that's not Lucy," sounding almost as if he wished it was. The DI did not, at that time, know that Bert had organised her kidnapping and knew, before he came to the station, that she was very much alive. He questioned the DI as to why they thought it could have been his wife and from where she had gone missing but the DI refused to give him any information. He asked Bert, as he had come down to see if it was Lucy, when was the last time he had seen his wife. Bert, not realising that the DI had access to the divorce papers, said that she had told him that she was going away for a few days with friends and would be back the following weekend. "I did not know where she was going and as the corpse is not her she could be anywhere. I will get her to get in touch when she returns so that you know that she is safe. I am due back at the barracks tomorrow morning so if you want to get in touch again that is where I shall be." DS Jones listening to the conversation and observing Bert's demeanour felt that he was not telling the truth and should be watched.

CHAPTER FIFTEEN

More Information

The superintendent brought the DI up to speed and requested that he go back to the hotel and speak to the manager again. On returning to the hotel on Wednesday morning the DI learned that Ryan Jones, the hotel chef, had owned up to regularly giving left overs to an old friend who would collect them in a suitcase. Having obtained his name and address they set out to interview him. Joe Goode, an old age pensioner, lived in a small cottage at the edge of the woods from where he watched the comings and goings of locals and visitors alike. He had been getting a little food, from his friend the chef, for as long as he could remember. He called to the hotel about once a week and got bits and pieces that would otherwise have been thrown out. On seeing the small suitcase, which he carried the food in, it was obvious that it was not the one described by the lady in the hotel. They were about to leave when the DI thought that Mr Goode may have seen something out of the ordinary on the weekend of the murder or on the weekend before when the birdwatchers were in the woods. "What are the weekends like" he asked Mr Goode, "are they noisy and do you see more people than usual? Did you notice anything different last weekend?" Mr Goode replied, "The weekend before last was the night of the full moon and it is always somewhat different. The group in fancy dress passed by as usual as they do each month on the night of the full moon, a little later than usual but as noisy as ever. They always dress up on that night, about twelve or fourteen of them, both men and women by the sound of their voices. They wear very impressive costumes and all of them have the head of an animal giving them an eerie look in the moonlight." The DI asked him if he would be nervous or afraid of them. "Oh no" he replied "they have been passing here for a long time now and I believe they just want to be different as they enjoy a few drinks and have some fun. I never hear them returning so assume they go home a different way." "What about the weekend just gone," the DI asked, "did you notice anything out of the ordinary." "If Monday morning counts I saw a man and a woman walking up towards the car park," The DI was a little amused at this and asked him what was unusual about that. "Oh I'm sorry it was very early and still dark but as a red car had driven up much earlier, about two-thirty if I remember correctly, I thought that perhaps they were meeting up in the carpark." "Could you describe the car or the man and woman?" he asked him. "Well I know the car was red because my security lights came on as it passed but I did not get a good look at the people." He heard Jack saying, "Did you notice what make of car it was or did you see the registration?" "Sergeant at that hour of the morning I was lucky to see the car." "Thanks Mr Goode you have been an immense help and hopefully we will not have to bother you again." As soon as he was sure that they had left Mr Goode made a phone call relating what he had just experienced. "Thanks for that information Joe, it may come in useful if they ever get around, which I doubt, to interviewing me."

Back at the station they began to wonder if things would ever come together. They had a crime scene, an unidentified body, a handbag with very few contents and a red car which may or may not be connected to the crime. They were missing the car owner, a man seen with her and possibly another woman. They had still failed to contact the two ladies from June Thompson's hike group and was it possible that there was a connection between Patrick Jones and Pauline Smith who DS Tobin had seen together in the woods? They wondered should they contact the bird watchers' group as they may have also been in the woods that night and seen or heard something. Joining them the superintendent was disappointed at how slowly things were progressing but was aware that until they could identify the body in the morgue finding the culprit would be difficult. She suggested interviewing and checking the alibis of those they had already spoken to. The DI told her about the fancy-dress group and she wondered could they identify some of them. He also told her of the red car driving to the carpark on Monday morning and the couple that followed later on. The super told them to call it a day and suggested that a fresh start could be made the following morning.

Thinking of that evening brought back memories, to the DI, unrelated to the murder but vivid in his mind. That was the evening that his daughter Cathy had told him that David, her boyfriend, wished to speak to him. With his mind preoccupied with thoughts of the murder investigation he was totally unprepared for the conversation that ensued. As soon as he saw David he realised that he was nervous and wondered what he wished to have a conversation about. He had never visualised being asked to give his consent to allow his Cathy to marry someone and was so taken aback by the request that for a moment he was speechless. All thoughts of the investigation were forgotten as he returned to the sitting room with a much-relieved young man and they joined Cathy and Elizabeth in a glass of champagne to celebrate their engagement. In a matter of minutes his son Edward arrived along with Emma his girlfriend and with what seemed like some form of telepathy his youngest daughters Julie and Hannah also appeared. He did not know that Elizabeth had told them earlier about the engagement and had asked them to join in the celebrations. It was a very happy occasion and lovely that the whole family could celebrate together.

CHAPTER SIXTEEN

Superintendent Checks On Charlotte

The following day, Thursday, the super arriving at the station decided to contact the international division and air her concerns about Charlotte. She explained that she did not believe her story that the group were collecting for charity and felt that when she was interviewing Charlotte that she had something to hide. Being asked to attend a meeting with her counterpart in the international division, that very afternoon, came as a great shock to her and she wondered had she stumbled on something important. She never expected the turn it took. "Superintendent you may have disturbed a hornet's nest and put Charlotte Robinson's life in danger. DS Robinson is our undercover officer and is only barely surviving as it stands. This now means that she will have to be watched and protected every minute from now on. We are at a critical point in our investigation and hope, with the help of the Dutch police, to have a positive outcome very soon. We are aware of a substantial amount of cash being brought to Amsterdam and what transpires will be closely watched by the authorities there. Any contact by you or your officers could spell her death warrant so ensure that your officers are fully aware of this and do not make any attempt to communicate with her. Back at the station while making this announcement the superintendent watched Jack closely and wondered what was going through his mind. She was surprised not to see much reaction and thought that perhaps he had known already. Jack found it hard to understand or believe what he had just heard and it was the shock of it that left him showing no response. He found it impossible to believe that she was also a member of the force and was devastated as he realised that he would not be able to meet her again until this was all over. He could not even speculate on how she must be feeling. That Charlotte was involved with the Gardai had never entered his mind and he was finding the news very difficult to come to terms with. How would that effect their newly found relationship? Would discussing cases become their main talking point or could they just have a normal conversation as before? Having a similar job would lend itself to them understanding each other's problems but was that really what he wanted? That she could be anything other than the beautiful, intelligent sophisticated girl, that he was in love with, was something that he could not cope with. Overcoming the initial shock he calmed down and appreciated that the news had not changed either of them and when next they got together they would still be in love and nothing else would matter.

CHAPTER SEVENTEEN

Luke Having Doubts

On that same day Luke was getting worried, this is what he had worked for throughout the past eight months. All he could think of was had he everything laid out correctly, had he covered his tracks completely, had the other group members, unaware of what was really going on, noticed anything suspicious? Things were beginning to build up as the trip to Amsterdam came closer. The final trip was not far away and there was so much still to do. He needed Margaret to spend a night with him on the yacht and help him to relax. Margret was the brains behind this operation and when tensions were high she and Luke often spent a night on board together. Their lovemaking made life bearable and they both relished the nights they spent together. No one in the group knew of their close relationship and none of them suspected that Margaret was the real leader. Everyone believed that Luke was in charge and it suited them to leave it that way. Ringing her and planning their night together brought a certain amount of relief but until she was aboard the yacht he would be apprehensive. Margaret lived in a secluded cottage, in the valley, about three miles from the town and not wishing her car to be seen on the quayside she felt it would be prudent for her to drive to the casino and park it there. She would then walk to the harbour where the yacht was berthed and join Luke. She spent part of the day putting her files in the safe as she could not afford for them to be seen should she have unexpected visitors. Living in this quiet corner of the forest she seldom saw anybody except passing hikers on the opposite side of the valley. This suited her perfectly as she needed peace and quiet when planning the group's operations. She was looking forward to her overnight stay with Luke and knew it would leave her relaxed and ready to set out the final plans for Amsterdam. On board they enjoyed a meal prepared by Luke and a bottle of sparkling wine which left them in a happy frame of mind as they settled down to a night of passion. As these nights did not happen very often it made them all the more exciting. The yacht was warm and comfortable as they took their time indulging in a period of restrained hugging and kissing, knowing that their love making would be explosive and beautiful. Their senses reeling, their bodies longing for each other, they slowly slipped out of their clothes and lay under the cool silk sheets. Their experience, which they had both been anticipating with relish, was once again beyond their expectations and as they lay together wondered why it did not happen more often. Friday morning came too soon but they woke up totally refreshed and focused on what still had to be done. With only three weeks to go, before the final payment was due and the arrival of the goods from Amsterdam, they needed to put the final plans in place. It had been a difficult year organising so much while working under the pretence of being a charitable organisation. They believed they had convinced the others but would be happy to see it come to an end. Charlotte had delivered the tickets to Gareth on time but for some reason he was not sure of her. Since seeing her being brought to the Garda station he had thought about her a lot. He felt her questions were more inquisitive than necessary but he had been so busy he had not focused on her at all. She was one more item that he would have to attend to very soon. Before leaving the yacht, they spent some time discussing how they would proceed and what information they would release to the group at the next meeting. Making sure the quay was clear Margaret slipped silently off the yacht and made her way back to her car. Luke tidied up and made sure that everything was back in its proper place. A last-minute check and he organised a lift back to the casino.

  Their nights of unrestraint lovemaking kept him going during the tough times and he felt that he owed Margaret big time. He would not let anything happen to her at any cost. Her cottage was a perfect hideaway and Margaret did most of the planning there and it was also a safe house if he needed to shield some of his friends. Arriving home he became agitated once again, as he continued to worry about Amsterdam. It was only himself, Margaret, Jim and Gareth who knew what was actually going on and doubts were forming about their reliability. Impossible to settle down things began to get the better of him and his thoughts were all over the place. Gareth had been chosen to travel to Amsterdam but had been acting strangely lately and he was not sure if he could be trusted with such a large amount of cash. Charlotte who he believed thought it was a fund-raising group was also causing him some concern. He wondered if she had really been called to the Garda station in connection with her bird watching activities. He had forgotten that she had told him that her interview had revolved around her involvement with a charitable organisation. He could not relax and his head began to fill up with more doubts. Charlotte, Charlotte, Charlotte kept vibrating across his brain as he tried to control his emotions. What was it about her that he could not come to terms with? Was her involvement with the bird watchers' group what it seemed? What was it that attracted her to his group? He could not remember who had recommended her or where she had come from. As he became increasingly more agitated he started to imagine that everyone in the group was conspiring against him. What could he do at this late stage? Should he have a meeting with Margaret, Jim and Gareth? Perhaps he should have a talk with Charlotte and dismiss his fears about her? Thinking of Charlotte he wondered if he had an underlying attraction for her which had prevented him from questioning her motives before now. He felt that Mark, Mary and Tina believed they belonged to a legitimate group and up until now had not worried about them but in his present state of mind they also seemed a threat. With his brain now overpowered by uncertainty he found it impossible to come to a decision. He decided he needed a few drinks and headed out to the local bar and ordered a large whiskey. Unfortunately, in his condition, he had forgotten how whiskey affected him and instead of becoming relaxed he got more agitated and his mind would not allow him to conceive a plan to ensure the success of his crooked venture. He believed that he would have to get hold of Charlotte, as a matter of urgency, and find some way to remove her from the scene until the operation was completed. He thought of bringing her to Margaret's cottage on the pretence of collecting some cash and leave her there until things were sorted out. Margaret would understand and be the perfect hostess. Gareth would be a different challenge as he was part of the team and along with Jim would be required to see the deal completed. His thoughts continued to distract him to a point where he was unable to put anything together. Not knowing what to do or where to go he believed that if he had a few more drinks his head would clear and he could get on with putting everything in order. This of course did not happen and in an intoxicated state he staggered home and fell into a deep sleep. Had Luke remained sober and thought things through he may have remembered that Mark had been very quiet recently and had been advocating that he and not Gareth should go to Amsterdam with the cash. Although Gareth and Mark were secretly planning together each had their own agenda for wishing to take the cash to Holland. Mark, who had many contacts, felt that it would be more beneficial for them both if he went as he thought that Gareth was not planning on him being in his final plans. To ensure his own destiny he made a few phone calls and tried to cover all possibilities. As he already belonged to an international smuggling consortium he never doubted his ability to out think Gareth and knew whatever was done he would find out about it very quickly. The network was spread far and wide and he was satisfied that where ever Gareth would go he would be found. If Gareth did abandon him it would cost him dearly. They had been planning this deception for many months but lately he feared that Gareth was heading in a new direction. Mark, through his contacts, was aware of Gareth checking out diamond dealers and knew that there were far more dangerous individuals who were also aware of his plans and would have no hesitation taking them from him even if it meant murdering him. Unknown to Gareth he had, for a long time, been smuggling diamonds and had already learned of Gareth's escape plan. If it did turn out that he was not included in his plans he would know where he was in a matter of days. In some ways he felt sorry for Gareth as he knew that all he wanted to do was to live a peaceful life but did not realise that the plan he had thought out would not work. There were too many others out there with the same ideas who, with a circle of contacts, would know his every move as soon as he made them. He would be lucky if he even got to sell the diamonds never mind keep the cash.

CHAPTER EIGHTEEN
Charlotte Feeling Vulnerable

Charlotte, still worried about the turn of events, wondered if she should confide in Jack. She knew that she would need somebody if things got nastier and believed that he would be her best ally. If it was discovered that she had gone against orders it would not be dealt with kindly and would certainly not help her promotion prospects in the future. Believing that Luke was getting suspicious made her nervous and she finally decided to call Jack. Using a call box, instead of her mobile, she told him of her fears. They could not be seen together so they arranged to meet at the fire hollow in the forest. This was fraught with danger and they both took every possible precaution as they made their way to the woods. At meeting they were both wary and it took some time before she was able to explain everything to him. She was aware of the yacht and gave him a full description and where it was moored. Margaret's house was a well-kept secret but she had followed her there one day and was able to give Jack all the details and directions. She told him that she would ring at midday and at six each evening but he need not answer. She would continue to use a public phone in case her mobile was being monitored. She felt if she was to have a problem, with Luke, she would end up on the yacht or hidden away in Margaret's house. "If I fail to ring you twice you will have to consider that something has gone wrong. At that point try ringing me and if I do not answer you can be sure that things are serious. I will try to give some indication of my position depending on which location that I end up in." The situation was serious and neither of them felt like staying together for too long. They went their separate ways Jack wishing he could stay with her and Charlotte hoping he would be there if she needed him. On her way out of the forest Charlotte met a few members of the bird watchers' group who had been photographing new nests and were on their way home. She was delighted to continue with them as this gave her a reason, if needed, for being there. The two officers, assigned to watching her movements, were surprised when they saw her leaving her house and heading in the direction of the woods. They kept her under observation from the house until she reached the edge of the forest. They remained under cover along the forest track but got distracted when they heard voices and lost sight of her. Checking from a distance they began to relax as they realised that is was some members of the bird watchers' group that they had heard and assumed that was the reason for her being there. Seeing Jack, as they continued to look for her, gave rise for concern and they followed him thinking he would lead them to her. Seeing them meeting, without any sign of intimacy, they concluded that something serious had occurred and they would have to intervene. Before getting a chance to do so they received an urgent message and knowing that she was in no immediate danger they returned to their car. This would have to be reported as soon as they dealt with the incident. Neither Jack nor Charlotte realised that they had been followed but both returned home with their own set of worries. Charlotte was fearful that she may have been spotted by her fellow Gardai and on the other hand she worried of the danger she could be in by belonging to the charity fund raising group. The thoughts of being found out by the group far outweighed her fear of repercussion at work. If Luke did doubt her intentions how would she handle it? Getting it into his head that she was anything but a volunteer could spell disaster for the continuation of her surveillance and put her in real danger. Margaret she thought was already suspicious and as the brains behind the operation could also cause serious consequences for the completion of her Garda operation. Realising that she should have thought this through before contacting Jack and putting him in danger she decided that she needed to rectify things. Ringing her superintendent she explained what she had done and asked for her advice. As it was getting late the super suggested meeting at the station first thing in the morning. Charlotte agreed to do this and hanging up felt very relieved. In the meantime Jack, sitting at home drinking a beer, began to formulate a plan to protect Charlotte. He would have to work things out while still concentrating on the murder investigation. He could not sit back waiting for her to call each day as this may not give him the chance of helping her if things got awkward. He would have to think of something clever but as usual when it is needed most things have a habit of not going to plan. He recalled her telling him the location of the yacht and thought that he would check it out the following morning. The cottage in the valley was a more challenging task but he would leave thinking about that until he had located the yacht. The following morning, Sunday, he drove to the harbour to find a yacht named the Morning Star. It was moored exactly as Charlotte had described so he parked his car nearby and casually walked along the quayside. Seeing the yacht so close he realised that it was motorised and powerful and could easily cross to Holland. Should Charlotte be taken on board it would be almost impossible for him to rescue her. He would have to make sure that he could intervene before that happened. Walking back to his car he tried to think what he would do if the occasion arose. His thoughts were disturbed as he spotted a car speeding towards and stopping at the yacht. A man unknown to Jack came off the yacht and got into the car before it made a fast turn and headed back towards the town. He took note of the registration number with the intention of checking it when he was back in the station. Satisfied that he had done everything he could he set out for the carpark at the edge of the woods. He put on his hiking boots and leaving the car he headed in to the forest, in the direction of the valley, where he hoped to find the cottage. Suddenly his phone rang and startled him, he had forgotten that Charlotte said that she would ring at noon. He could see that it was Charlotte and did not answer as agreed. Then he realised that if he could see her name she was not using a public phone and he could not understand why she was using her mobile. He decided to send her a quick text and just wrote "Are you OK." His phone rang again and this time he answered it. He heard her say, "Jack, there is no need for us to stay connected as your help will not now be needed. I have just finished a meeting with my superintendent where I was informed that last night we had been followed to the hollow by undercover Gardai. I had not realised that I was being protected around the clock. Please leave everything lie for a couple of weeks and when this is all tied up we can get together again." "Oh boy can I expect a grilling when I get back to the station." Charlotte told him that he need not worry on that score as she had been assured that it would be safer for everyone if his part in all of this was not disclosed, even to his superintendent, as this information could jeopardise the whole operation. "At this moment all I can say is a million thanks for all you have done but I will enjoy making it up to you the next time we are together." Quickly hanging up she left Jack bewildered. What should he do? Before this is all over there may be an opportunity for him to help her. He decided to continue his walk into the forest and hope that he might find something that may prove useful. Nearing the end of the ridge he looked across the valley and observed a cottage barely visible among the gorse and heather. It looked deserted but from that distance he could not be sure. Making a note of his surroundings he headed back towards the carpark. It was a lovely sunny day in a picturesque area so he stopped quite often and took some photographs. Stepping back off the track to get a better view he stood on an unusual object. Seeing a rolling pin in the middle of a forest was mystifying until he remembered that the murdered woman had been hit with a blunt instrument. He rang DI Brown and told him of his find. A forensic team was dispatched immediately and Jack knew not to touch anything and to remain at the scene until they arrived. If it turned out to be the weapon used it might indicate the direction that the assailant took following the murder. As it was his day off Jack left the team to complete their work and went home. On Monday morning Dr Taylor confirmed that the size, shape and weight of the rolling pin was consistent with the injuries sustained by the victim. Being out in the elements, for so long, had removed any hope of finding fingerprints. The team had taken photographs of footprints mainly because they belong to a pair of shoes and not hiking boots which would be unusual for anyone walking along that mountain track. Now there was a corpse, a possible murder weapon but they were still no nearer to solving the crime.

CHAPTER NINETEEN

New Challenge In The Murder Investigation

Two weeks into the investigation and it was still at a standstill. Following instructions Jack had not been in touch with Charlotte but missed her terribly and worried for her safety. Thinking of Charlotte he remembered he had not followed up on seeing Patrick Jones in the forest with Pauline Smith. Should he call to Patrick and ask him or should he approach Pauline Smith? The Jones's house was closest so that is where he headed for and as he arrived a motorbike was preparing to leave. On seeing Jack Pauline stopped and greeted him. Patrick was at the door and as she left she called back "see you later Dad." One problem solved without a single question being asked. He could see that Patrick was waiting for him to explain his presence there but all he could think of asking him was had he remembered anything else from the morning he found the body. "No not a thing if I do I'll let you know." Jack could not explain what it was that made him feel that Patrick was hiding something each time he spoke to him. That afternoon there was a report of a woman in her thirties missing in Galway. She had gone to complete a two-week course on mountain safety including a map and compass course and had not returned home. Her parents believed that she was camping somewhere with a friend but offered to come down and try to identify the body. Mr and Mrs Penny were brought from their home in Galway by Gardai and following a conversation with the DI agreed to go to the morgue. The description they gave of their daughter did not match the body found in the woods and they hoped that it was somebody else. A sigh of relief from both of them as they confirmed that it was not their missing daughter, leaving the DI no better off than before they arrived. What might be a break in the case came on Tuesday morning. As the DI arrived at the station he was approached by a gentleman who asked to have a word with him. Going into his office with this complete stranger he wondered if it had anything to do with the investigation. Stephen Cloak sat down and said that his being there had nothing to do with the murder but as he and his friends had been in the woods the previous weekend he felt that he should explain the reason for them being there. He told the DI that they were a group of friends who dressed up each month on the night of the full moon to enjoy a few drinks and a laugh in the woods. We usually meet in a hollow where we can light a fire but on that night there were a number of people already there when we arrived. I watched them for a while but when I saw them lighting a fire I decided to move and have our drinks elsewhere. I would not have bothered you but there was one unidentified person in the group that night and we have still not found out who she was. We all wear the head of some animal and part of the fun is trying to discover who is behind the mask. It is a mixed group of unmarried people and we engage in some adult practices not knowing who our partner for the night will be. It was only yesterday that I learned that Joseph Kelly, one of our group, had been partnered with this unknown lady. I can give you the names of all the members but I have no idea who this other person was. The DI took all the details and asked him to get Joseph Kelly to call in to see him. This he agreed to do and went on his way. The DI wondered why he had come in to the station himself and had not just asked Joseph Kelly instead. He knew that it was a week before the murder so why did he think it mattered? Did he know something that he did not reveal? Would he have been in the forest on the weekend of the murder and had seen something? Did he believe that Joseph Kelly knew something that might be useful? Would he have been meeting this lady again? Was this lady the corpse they had in the morgue? He was wondering was he just clutching at straws as, at that moment, he had no idea how things were turning out. Having an unidentified body was really frustrating as without knowing who she was made it impossible to establish a motive or to have any idea of her movements prior to the murder. Joseph Kelly was surprised when he was asked to call to the Garda station. Stephen Cloak had not told him that he had been speaking to the DI, only that he was asked to tell him to call to the station. It never dawned on him that it could be connected to the murder and was somewhat puzzled at the request. On arrival at the station on Wednesday morning he was escorted to the DI'S office where he was asked about his association with the fancy-dress group. Not knowing why he was being asked about this caught him off guard and he was not sure how to react. Becoming defensive he said that he had done nothing wrong and as far as he knew there was no law against wearing fancy dress. The DI, sensing his embarrassment, asked him if he knew the identity of the lady he had been with on the last night of the full moon. "Yes of course I do but why would you want to know about her." He heard the DI say, " We are trying to establish the whereabouts of anybody that may be missing and that lady, according to Stephen Cloak, could not be traced or identified." Replying he said, "Inspector the reason that nobody in the group got to know her was because she is my girlfriend and she did not wish to get involved, on that night, with anybody else. Her name is Sophie Henderson and I can call her now for you to confirm her identity. I would appreciate her name not being given to other members of the group." The DI spoke to her for a few minutes and afterwards told Jim that there was no reason, that he could see, to disclose her name to anyone. Was it just curiosity that Stephen Cloak had brought this to his attention or was there something else bothering him? I shall need to speak to him again soon. Was this another dead end to the investigation?

CHAPTER TWENTY

Lucy Rescued

It was over two weeks since Lucy had ended up in the cottage and she was beginning to wonder why Bert had not come back. She had not been eating a lot so the food in the fridge had lasted well. She had reached the point of knowing that if he did not turn up soon it would be impossible for her to stay there any longer and she would have to break out no matter what the cost. Had he decided to just leave her there and not bother coming back? She had never expected to be left for so long. Relaxing on the sofa she was aware of a car pulling into the driveway and jumped up expecting to see him open the door. Not hearing the door open she looked out the window only to see a post van parked there. She watched a while before getting the courage to knock loudly on the window. The post lady, who had pulled in off the road for a quick break, could not believe that there was someone in the house. Going cautiously to the window she listened as Lucy asked her to call the Gardai. The local Garda station was only a mile away and a patrol car was with them in minutes. Once they had established who Lucy was they asked her to open the door so that they could look after her. The door was locked and they were forced to break in. Although Bert had said that the house was alarmed none went off. The Gardai knew of her being missing but could not believe that she had been kidnapped and held so close to them for all that time. They were delighted to inform the DI of her release and drove her back to the Garda station where the DI learned of her husband kidnapping her. She went back to the hotel where she received a huge welcome. No information of her release was made and a watch was maintained at the cottage for Bert's return. The DI got in touch with his commanding officer who explained that Bert had been accidently shot on the firing range. He had received a head wound ten days earlier and had been kept in an induced coma in the military hospital. Explaining about the kidnapping the DI requested that he be allowed to speak to him when he recovered. In typical military fashion he was assured that he would be informed when Bert was fit enough to be interviewed. When he relayed the news to Lucy she simply acknowledged the reason for him not returning to the cottage but wondered why she had not been advised of his accident by his CO. She knew that the authorities were aware of the divorce proceedings but she was still his wife and should have been informed. Receiving a reply to her enquiry, from his CO, she learned that an officer had called to her house and not getting an answer had written a letter of explanation and posted it to her. On receiving this information she realised that she had been at the cottage during that time and had not been home since. She wondered how badly had he been injured and hoped it would not make the divorce proceedings any harder. She was not really interested in how he was other than that it might interfere with her plans. Ringing the CO she requested permission to visit him. She was told that he was still in an induced coma but as his wife they would allow her to see him. She could not believe that the person she was being shown was Bert. He was lying there, without a movement, he could have been dead and she hardly recognised him. She knew that she would not go back to see him again and would proceed with the divorce as planned. She thought that he had received what he deserved and had no sympathy for him at all. What the future held for her she had no idea but believed it could be no worse than it had been living with him.

CHAPTER TWENTY-ONE

Repeat Interviews

It was agreed to repeat interviews and so on Friday, with very little to go on, the DI set about speaking to everyone again. He interviewed those who DS Tobin had spoken to and he sent Jack to see the others. Another change of story came from Declan O'Grady who now admitted to having gone for a walk when they closed the shop at six that evening. He had failed to mention it at the earlier interview. He may not have considered it important but it did put him in the forest within the time frame of the murder. A lady walking alone had not been noticed by anyone. Most accounts of the day remained the same but arriving at the café he thought that there seemed to be some tension between Anthony and Betty Gleeson and he wondered if it had anything to do with Anthony having said that Betty had been away that Sunday. He now admitted that he knew that she was hiking locally with her friend Emily and although he had denied being out himself he told the DI that he did have a walk early that morning. Did he believe that she knew something or was he concealing a secret himself? Perhaps she had found out about his early morning meetings with Amelia. The DS called to see Patrick Jones and seeing his wife using a rolling pin reminded him of the one he had found in the forest. None of the people that he spoke to could add to their story and nobody had encountered a lone lady out walking. Mrs Jones, who had not previously been interviewed, said she went out most mornings collecting herbs and wild berries for her baking. She had not seen any strangers but had observed Patrick, her husband, talking to a woman. When asked could she describe what she looked like or what she was wearing answered that she only saw them in the distance. Checking notes, with the DI back at the station they wondered if Amelia Jones, who had earlier said that she thought her husband might be seeing another woman, had deliberately followed him to see was he meeting someone. Another thought was if she and Anthony Gleeson were seeing each other secretly that might account for him not saying that he had been out walking. Perhaps Declan O'Grady also had a secret which he could not afford his wife to find out about. It had been a long day so they finished up with the thoughts of making a fresh start the following morning. As they prepared to leave the DI was reminded that his wife had rung and asked that he get in touch with her before heading home. On ringing her he learned that their son Edward had been promoted and both he and Emma his girlfriend were calling to see them. She asked him to go to the shop and pick up a few things on his way home. He was delighted to hear that Edward, an electrical engineer with the defence forces, had finally got his promotion as Emma, serving with the navy, had been promoted to the rank of third engineer and Edward had hoped his promotion would come through. Another evening when all the family appeared from nowhere and celebrated together. Hannah and Julie where intrigued on hearing that they had met when Edward did a tour of the naval vessel which was on a courtesy visit to the port. Emma told them that she had been assigned to showing visitors around and answering any queries. She had been delighted when Edward asked her some electrical questions as most of the visitors were only interested in the size of the ship and the ports they travelled to. She told them that she had felt an immediate attraction but did not think herself lucky enough to expect him to feel the same way. As they reached the end he had complimented her on the manner in which she had conducted the tour and to her delight asked her if she would like them to go for a drink together. This had happened about eighteen months previous and they were still getting on fine. It was a great family celebration and went on much later than usual. Saturday, started at the station, with a phone call from Angela Winters who had been requested by her local Gardai to get in touch. She explained that she had been on holidays and had not even heard of the murder. Her friend Joan was spending some time with her ill mother but would ring them if needed. When asked about travelling home following their hike with June Thompson she told him that they had a car that day and drove home following a cup of coffee in the café where they had met that morning. She did not think they had spoken to anyone other than the hike group and did not remember seeing anyone walking alone. Where Patrick and Amelia Jones conspiring together to give the impression that there was a lady walking alone while in fact there was only one lady in the woods and she was now lying in the morgue? Did Patrick, knowing how the murdered woman was dressed, deliberately give a false account of the type of clothes being worn by that other woman? Was it a coincidence that both women were not suitably dressed for the cold weather or walking in the hills? Was there a chance, that if there had been two ladies, that they would have started out together and if so how did they arrive at that spot in the forest? Would one of them have driven off and taken the bag and keys with her? There were so many questions to be answered and very few leads to follow. Sunday and it was the night of the full moon once again and as the DI was anxious to speak to the fancy-dress group he decided that this was a good chance to see them all together. He waited, with DS Tobin, outside Mr Goode's cottage and stopped them as they came by. They were not happy with this intrusion on their night out and indicated that it would spoil their fun if they knew who was behind the mask before they even got started. The DI reminded them that it was a murder enquiry but told them that he had envisaged this situation and had a plan all prepared but if they preferred they could all come down to the station for their interviews. Not wishing to do this they agreed to his request and stayed there. He took them, one at a time, away from the group leaving Jack to ensure that the others remained. Remembering that Mr Cloak had told him it was a mixed group of single people he was taken aback seeing Amelia Jones and Anthony Gleeson among them. They all denied having been in the woods at the time of the murder and said that they only met once a month on the night of the full moon. Mr Cloak was not with them so the DI decided he would have to interview him another time. Leaving them to their partying he and Jack went home without any breakthrough in the case. Neither Anthony nor Amelia could believe what had happened, they had been interviewed separately but were worried that it would get back to their families. They realised that they would not have been seen as being together but as the only married people in the group they would stand out. As this could be the end of them getting together for a while they made the most of it and paired off as soon as they arrived at the hollow. Nobody was supposed to know who was behind the mask but they could not afford to end up with someone else and had their own way of recognising each other. A simple plan was all that was necessary, they used florescent laces in their shoes which could be picked out quite easily. There was an urgency about their lovemaking that night, both realising that it may be their last night together for a long time. Angela Winters was contacted on Monday morning and asked to get Joan Davis to ring the DI. The following day a call from her was received at the Garda station. She explained that she was looking after her mother who had been ill for some time but would come down to the station if required.

CHAPTER TWENTY-TWO

Weekly Meeting At The Casino

The Midweek meeting at the casino was following its usual course, starting with the minutes of the previous meeting and then following a set agenda. Each of the participants gave an account of their individual collections and their plans for the following four weeks. Luke reminded them that there was less than two weeks left for this particular charity collection but they would be given all the information on the new charity drive at the next meeting. Any cash promised but not collected would be put into the next venture. Last item was any other business and Luke used this to remind everyone for the necessity of secrecy until their charity partners in Holland actually received the cash. He questioned Gareth about the travel arrangements and got assurance from Joseph about the availability of a car. He knew that Mark was just a volunteer but not wanting him to get suspicious asked him to be available in case he was needed. Turning to the ladies he complimented them on their tremendous contribution and thanked them for all their hard work. Turning to Charlotte he asked her to meet him the following day as he had some cash to collect and thought that she would be the ideal person to help him. She agreed thinking that it might lead to her learning some valuable information. The meeting finished but Luke and Margaret remained behind dealing with some things they could not discuss in front of the others. They both agreed that Charlotte could be a threat but neither knew why. They felt that if they could keep her busy at the cottage, updating the accounts, she would not have time to interfere with their plans. Margaret did not think keeping her at the cottage overnight was a good idea especially if she was not what she claimed to be. Margaret had hundreds of invoices which would keep Charlotte busy for days. They hoped they could be sure that Gareth would deliver the cash to Amsterdam. They knew it was a lot to trust him with but he had the air tickets and had never let them down before. Margaret realised that it was their best option as they could not afford to be caught themselves with such a large amount of cash and ending up on the wrong side of the law. They agreed to let him take the risk knowing he was being well looked after. Mark, Jim and Gareth thought the meeting would never end. They, having heard of Bert Delaney's shooting accident, needed to get their ex-army buddies together for a briefing. Mark, although never having been in the army, knew of the comrade's secret and was included in all of their briefings. Not wishing to be seen together locally, they booked a small meeting room in a hotel some distance away. Kevin Burke and Colm O'Hara arrived early and had lunch together while waiting for Declan O'Grady. With Jim, Gareth and Mark they made their way to the meeting room where, all six of them, prepared to discuss a serious situation. Kevin Burke spoke first and they heard him say, " We find ourselves in a difficult place and will have to come to a group decision as to how we handle it. Three of our comrades are not here, Lena who is in the morgue, Bert because of his accident and Marge is absent as she had to remain and keep the shop open. Our main concern is Bert's condition and if it could lead to a breach in our solidarity. Another problem we have, is deciding whether it was an accident or an attempt on Bert's life. If he fails to get back his memory and continues not to remember our exploits all those years ago we will not have to worry. Recovering completely would also not be a problem as he would be true to our pledge and not ever speak of the past. The issues we may face if he regains his health slowly and haphazardly and speaks of our past, could be catastrophic for us all. At the moment my MP friends are monitoring him closely and will keep me advised of any change in his behaviour. On that score we can only wait and hope. Of greater concern is that he may have been shot on purpose and if that was the case we would have to figure out who the culprit was and why. We know that his wife is seeking a divorce but could not believe that she would have orchestrated something like this. With the recent murder of Lena Nowak we will have to consider the facts surrounding this tragedy. We were all there ten years ago when her brother Tobias died while we were all hunting with our comrades. Shortly afterwards her cousin Jakub Gorski, while serving, as a firing instructor, with the United Nations, introduced her to Antoni Nowak and they got married very quickly. He absconded shortly afterwards and has not been seen since. Bert Delaney was the best man at their wedding and I believe kept in touch after he disappeared. The day of the recent accident, when Bert was injured, the firing officer in charge was Jakub Gorski, her cousin, and although no blame has been put on him the situation lends itself to an investigation. Was he aware what happened all those years ago without us knowing? Did he think that Bert had something to do with his cousin Lena's death? Did he think that Bert had actually killed her? Would he be in contact with Lena's husband? Could this be some sort of reprisal?" He then asked them "Do you have any thoughts on the way forward." There was silence for a few minutes, as this information sank in, then everybody seemed to start speaking together. Jim, the loudest, could be heard above the others as he said, "If it was not an accident but committed on purpose and Jakub did not do it, must we think that someone else knows of our past and will either look to blackmail us, or will take his revenge by picking us off one by one." Declan spoke up and said "whoever was responsible, if it was on purpose, must still be in the forces or have very close links to it. An incident like that would have to be either well planned or created by an expert on the spur of the moment. As Jakub Gorski was on a special training mission he would not have known, in advance, that Bert was part of the group and if it was him, that committed the crime, I believe it was a decision taken at the last moment." Colm O'Hara could not believe that all they could think of was themselves and what might happen if the truth came out. "Have none of you the slightest interest in how our friend Bert, now lying ill in hospital, is feeling. He is the victim here, and although I do agree that we need to sort things out, surely our first thoughts must be on him and his recovery." Kevin spoke out again saying "Bert's recovery will be of no consequence if there is somebody out there with vengeance in their heart intending to make us pay for our misdoing. We must consider all elements surrounding our past, the murder of Lena Nowak and the shooting of Bert Delaney and see if there is a common denominator linking them together. Had Bert an opportunity to murder her and what, if he did, was his reason? Did he do it under orders from Jakub who then tried to silence him? Did he witness the murder and not realise that the killer had seen him? Was there someone else involved relating back to our early days and who believed it was time to make us pay? Could it be that it had been an unfortunate accident and we have nothing to fear? Logically the thing for us to do would be to wait until we hear the result of the C O's investigation into the accident and take it from there. The main issue with that is, if it turns out not to have been an accident, would the culprit be identified and named? I think we must resolve this now by drawing our own conclusions and acting accordingly." Kevin then addressed Jim and charged him with the task of keeping in touch with Bert and watching for whatever changes may appear in his health. He advised Colm to listen to all the train conversations that he could and ascertain what the general feeling relating to the murder was. He told Declan, who ran the newsagents, to read all reports given by the Gardai, through which they might pick up some valuable information. Knowing that Gareth and Mark were both involved with dealings outside the law he expected them to listen for any information that may not be available to the rest of them. He finished up by saying "I am going to catch up with Jakub before he returns home and hopefully gain some knowledge that we can put to our advantage." They left the room, at spaced intervals, and made their way home all wondering what lay in store for them. Declan, on arriving home, related everything to Marge who wondered had they been seen sheltering Lena the night before she was murdered. She had just appeared that night and she honestly had no idea who had called and taken her out early the following morning. Being involved with Declan and his army buddies could be trying but as she had been in the forces with them and was privy to the early days happenings she had no option but to remain. Thinking about how things were turning out she was convinced that there was a woman somehow involved but could not remember anybody other than Lena, now lying on a slab in the morgue, who would know what had happened all those years ago. Trying to reconstruct the incident in her head made her feel sick and she wished it had never happened. That it seemed to be the cause of their present-day problems made her very nervous and she knew there could be a lot more unrest to come. Why, she thought, was this happening now? Who outside the comrades knew of their past? Was it one of their own not able to cope with the memories? Was there anything she could do about it?

CHAPTER TWENTY-THREE

Frustration At The Garda Station

While that was the situation with the army comrades on Wednesday, a totally different scenario was playing out at the incident room in the Garda station. On Thursday morning the superintendent called an emergency meeting to discuss the progress in the murder investigation. She was being put under severe pressure by her superiors who believed that time was of the essence in solving a murder and wanted to see results. The DI's report was straight forward. He said that nothing had changed and there was still an unidentified body in the morgue. He also reminded them that neither Meg Walsh nor Jason O'Connor nor a possible second lady believed to be staying at the same address had been located. There was a reported loss of car keys and a list of fifteen people who could have been in the forest at the time of the murder. Several of the original statements had been amended which may or may not be of any value. The DI was concerned that the possible murder weapon, the rolling pin, which Jack had found in the forest so far away may not have been what they were looking for. Having spoken to Amelia Jones he felt that she, like her husband, was hiding something. The super, looking through her notes, realised that although they had received phone calls from both Angela Winters and Joan Davis they had not seen them in person. Neither had they seen Joseph Kelly's girlfriend Sophie Henderson. The

DI had not seen Michael Jones so added him to his list. The changes in some statements also gave her cause for concern. We will speak to those who changed their statements, advise those we have not seen to come into the station and interview anyone who could have been in the woods that weekend. While all this was going on DS Tobin was heading back to interview the shop owners totally unaware of the changing circumstances. As he passed the café he saw Charlotte having what looked like, a serious conversation with the man he had seen getting off the yacht. Alarm bells started to ring and he considered rushing in. Fortunately, the plain clothes Gardai, protecting her, saw him and advised him to leave it to them. Reluctantly he did as requested but remained, unnoticed, close by in case he was needed. Seeing her getting into a car he immediately moved forward but was restrained and could only watch as she was driven away. Going from shop to shop interviewing the owners had lost all sense of urgency and all he could think of was Charlotte. Where was she being brought to? Was it to the yacht and would she be taken out to sea and dumped overboard? Would he find her in the cottage being held prisoner by Margaret? He finally relaxed and convinced himself that she was being protected and got on with the task in hand. Having spoken to most of the owners on his list, and not learning anything new, He went over to see Patrick Jones. As he arrived at the house he heard raised voices and saw Patrick and Amelia arguing. Before they realised that he was there he overheard some of their conversation. "How do you know what she was wearing?" "I could not miss seeing such unsuitable attire." "Why where you there? Who were you seeing?" "That's none of your business." The talking stopped as they saw him and they invited him into the house as though nothing had happened. When asked about their original statements they both agreed that what they had said was all they could remember. He told Amelia that the superintendent would like to speak to her and asked her to call into the station. As he was leaving he turned and nonchalantly asked could he speak to Michael. Both of them got defensive and said that he was away doing a job for his firm. They had no idea where he was working but would ask him the next time they were speaking to him. Amelia agreed to call in to see the super and would let Michael know that the DI wished to speak to him. Jack, writing down what he had heard of the conversation earlier, was convinced that it was to do with the corpse in the morgue or the lone lady in the woods. Jack made his way back towards the cafe to interview Betty Gleeson but seeing the car that Charlotte had been driven away in, outside a pub, he made a detour and parked down the road. It was over two hours since she had left so he wondered why she would still be in the pub. Had they given her minders the slip? Two plain clothes Gardai were sitting in an unmarked car watching the bar entrance so Jack slipped in a side door. It was only a small country bar and it was immediately obvious that she was not there. He returned to his car and drove to the wharf to observe the yacht. It was unmoved since his last visit and looked deserted. His first thought was that she could be at the cottage and so he headed in the direction of the forest carpark. As he drove along the main street he was surprised to see Charlotte turning quickly and walk into the hairdressing saloon. Seeing her he realised how much he missed her and was tempted to break the rules and go over to her. Where had she been and was she all right? She had only gone in the door when his phone rang. All she said was "I will be with Snow White for the next few days" and hung up. Not being able to hold him close upset her greatly and she longed for them to be together again. She knew that she was being watched and could not be seen to be with him but her heart was telling her to go to him. Duty prevailed and like Jack she had to do what was expected of them. As she had used the phone in the saloon he knew that all was not right. He was lost for a moment to understand her short message but then realised that she was telling him that she would be at the cottage in the woods. He was not sure if she was looking for his help or, having seen him earlier, letting him know that she was all right. She obviously knew that she was being watched and could not use her own phone. He decided that he should advise her bodyguards but when he returned to the bar they were nowhere to be seen. As there was nothing more that he could do he went in to speak to Betty Gleeson. She told him that she had no idea why her husband had said she was away as he knew that she was showing her friend, Emily, the waterfall that day. She said that he had gone out walking very early that morning. At the time she thought he was getting some fresh air as he would be in the shop for the rest of the day, "He goes off alone late at night every now and then, I just put it down to his army background and him needing to get away from the shop and relax." "Your friend Emily, when would it be convenient to speak to her?" "She lives in the city but she will be out hiking with me again this weekend and I will bring her to the station then." Returning to the station all he could think of was what could he do to help Charlotte. He believed that she would have told him if she was in trouble and decided to wait and see how things turned out. He related what he had heard at the Jones house to the DI and was surprised that he did not see it as being significant. So Jack ended another day without progress. The DI had a similar day with one exception, Stephen Cloak could not recall where he had been that weekend. He remembered attending a farewell party for a work colleague on Friday night but had no memory of where he had been between then and Monday morning. Somewhere in the back of his mind he thought he had slept with someone but could not remember who she was. The DI reminded him that it was a murder enquiry and that his answer was not good enough. He advised him to talk to some of the other participants who attended the party and find out where he had been and who he had been with. He told him to return to the station the next day with the relevant information. His friends told that he had far too much to drink and they had left him back to his house where he had fallen asleep on the couch. Asking them about who he had been with they told him it was his imagination or a dream as no one would have gone anywhere with him in his drunken state.

CHAPTER TWENTY-FOUR

The Statement Changes

Superintendent Daly's first interview was with Anthony Gleeson. When asked, why he had not disclosed the fact that he had been in the hills, he said that he thought he was being asked had he been hiking during the day, with the hike group. She then asked him what time did he go out at and for how long was he in the woods. He said that he went out about eight and returned at nine thirty to open the shop. "Did you see anyone while you were there," "No he replied it was very quiet as usual at that hour of the morning," She then caught him off guard by asking him had he spoken to a friend, a lady perhaps? Thinking that Amelia must have told of their meeting and the super knew of this he admitted to having met Amelia Jones. A little annoyed he said that it did not seem relevant to him that his meeting a friend could have a bearing on the murder case. The super was quick to reply and advised him that she would be the judge of that. "Mr Gleeson you just give me the honest facts and I will decide what is or is not relevant." He had nothing else to say except that he had not encountered anybody else on his walk. "You may return to your shop now but it may be necessary, for us, to have a further conversation in the future." She felt that he was not telling the whole truth but accepted that it could be to do with meeting Amelia which he would not want his wife to know about. She thought that speaking to Betty

Gleeson might be interesting and informative. Declan O'Grady sauntered into the station and casually asked to speak to the superintendent. Going into her office he made it quite clear that he had nothing to do with murder and said that it would not do his business any good if his customers heard that he was being questioned about it. He was taken aback as he heard her say, "You would not be here Mr O'Grady if you had been upfront when you were speaking to DS Tobin. Your customers do not interest me and if you continue to make false statements you will find yourself here quite often." "Now," she continued, "perhaps you would like to tell me why you omitted to say that you were walking after six-thirty that evening." "Firstly," he replied, "it was a case of just forgetting as I was only out for a short time and secondly I do not know what it has to do with your investigation." He then remarked "You hardly think I am the murderer." Her answer was sharp and blunt as she told him that, although it may come as a surprise to him, until the killer is found everyone is a suspect especially those that were in the area at that time. Continuing she reminded him that as he had changed his statement he would most likely be questioned again. One more question she asked him was had he met anyone else during his walk. Reluctantly, he said he had spoken to some members of the local hike group as they returned from their walk but had not seen any strangers. She then finished the interview by telling him that he had given her the information she needed and advised him that further meetings may be required. As he left he saw Stephen Cloak sitting in DI Browne's office and wondered was he there for the same reason. Later that day, while talking to the DI, the superintendent asked him if he knew why people seemed to develop a guilt complex as soon as they entered a Garda station. "Possibly because they all have something to hide though not necessarily to do with what they are being questioned about." He told her that he had been speaking again to Mr Cloak, who had come in without being asked, and he did not know what to make of him. He felt that he wished to tell him something but did not know where to start. He thought, if he came in again, the super could speak to him and he may open up and tell her what was on his mind. There was no time to interview anyone else so anything outstanding had to wait until the following morning. Friday started with the arrival of Sophie Henderson and having seen her passport and thanking her for coming in, he escorted her to the door, hoping the rest of the day would be as beneficial. Before going out she turned to the DI and told him that she had been Stephen Cloak's girlfriend up to a few months earlier and she thought that was the reason for him trying to get Joseph Kelly involved in something that he had nothing to do with. She was sure that Stephen had known who she was and had deliberately gone out of his way to cause a rift between them. The DI now had some idea why Stephen Cloak had come to the station but still thought that he had something more which he needed to talk about. Now that he had a starting point he might be able to get him to talk about it.

CHAPTER TWENTY-FIVE
Charlotte's Dilemma

Jack was trying to concentrate on the investigation but could only think of Charlotte who, he knew, was being asked to work in the cottage every day which put her under severe pressure. She was fully aware that she was, deliberately, being kept from doing anything that would upset the plans for the coming weekend. She was convinced that they did not trust her anymore and wondered what had brought about this change. She worried about Luke as he had been making suggestions that she could save herself the journey to the cottage each day by working on the yacht. Saying this in front of Margaret, one morning, brought on quite a reaction and Charlotte suddenly realised that there was more to them that just the business. Margaret sensed that it was not work that Luke had in mind and had no intention of having competition. She was adamant that the books would have to be completed in the cottage and not on the yacht. Shortly afterwards, with Margaret out of sight, he invited her to share a meal on board. She put him off by saying that she had already planned for that evening but left it open that she could accept in a few days. She knew that she would never actually go with him but needed time to work out how she could avoid it. Her visits to the cottage were getting more strained as each day passed with Luke continuing to look for an answer. Realizing the feelings that Margaret had for Luke Charlotte thought that if she asked her advice, about visiting the yacht, she could prevent him from asking her again. Margaret gave the impression that it would not bother her but Charlotte knew by her demeanour that she was furious. Whatever was said between them Charlotte never found out but she was never asked again. That afternoon, while sifting through a box of invoices, Charlotte spotted a note relating to the purchase of diamonds due to be collected in Amsterdam. She was surprised at this, as up to now, they were only aware of the group handling drugs. Not wanting it known that she had seen it she put the note into a box that she would not be expected to check before the weekend. As she prepared to leave she overheard part of a phone conversation between Luke and Gareth which indicated that lobster pots would be dropped close to the coast on Sunday morning. She heard no more as she was afraid of being noticed but knew that both sets of information would be valuable. On Friday evening, as she was leaving, she told Margaret that she had no more time off work and could not come back on Monday morning. She felt that Margaret would have stopped her leaving if it had been possible but she was already out the door and there was no going back. She had learned a lot in the week at the cottage and knew she would have to be very alert at the Wednesday meeting if she was to remain safe and obtain any information of importance relating to the coming weekend.

CHAPTER TWENTY-SIX
Jason And Meg Return

Honeymoon over Jason and Meg returned home on Saturday to find a letter from Eva explaining about their car keys. They had arrived home by taxi but never even noticed that their car was not in the driveway. As they went to the window in disbelief they saw a garda car pull into their driveway. A Garda came over to them and having ascertained who they were, told them what had happened while they were away and advised them that their car was in the car compound. They wondered how they could collect their car without keys. The Garda explained about the forensic team getting a new set and they would now be available. They could not believe all that had happened while they were away but were very pleased that their car was safe. The Garda drove them to the station and they had a chat with the super and collected their car. After speaking to them and obtaining all the facts the Garda filed a report advising the DI of the latest events. There safe return changed everything and meant that some elements of the case could be discarded. At last now they were able to remove the possibility of Jason and Meg being in any way involved with the murder but they were still left with an unidentified corpse.

CHAPTER TWENTY-SEVEN
The Next Stage

A fresh approach was now needed so a revision of all the evidence began. An unidentified corpse still lay in the morgue and except for the return of Jason and Meg nothing else had changed. No new evidence had presented itself so things remained at a standstill. It was now important to get a positive identification of Angela Winters and Joan Davis two hikers from June Thompson's group who, although they had spoken by phone had never come to the station. It was also possible that some unknown people had hiked across the hills without being seen. The couple seen by Mr Goode had never been looked for and the lone lady in the forest, reported by Patrick Jones, had never been located. Several hours were spent discussing the evidence but to no avail and it was believed, that without new leads, they would continue to go around in circles. The superintendent was getting tired and impatient so suggested an adjournment. Jacks' thoughts were on Charlotte and not on the discussion so he almost missed hearing that they were finishing up for the night. Following the meeting Jack met his friend William and enjoyed a few relaxing drinks. Being a Garda detective he was interested in hearing how the investigation was progressing and part of their conversation centred around the murder. Learning of the handbag being found in the casino bar reminded him of a similar occurrence a few months earlier when he believed the barman was involved but could not find evidence to prove it. He promised to ask his friends, who frequented the bar, if they had heard anything relating to the bag being found. On his way home, following the adjournment, DI Browne spotted Hannah and Julie at a bus stop and stopped to give them a lift home. They were delighted with this as they had taken a lift from a fellow student who, remembering he had promised to meet a friend, left them at the bus stop. They were both in their final college year with Hannah completing a course in social studies and Julie studying English literature and French. They hoped to graduate together and before taking up any positions they were making plans to tour around Europe for a few months. It always amazed him to see how different they were and yet got on so well together. All the way home their conversation centred around travel arrangements, the countries they would like to visit and of course on the clothes they had bought. Although twins they looked and acted totally differently and their choice in clothes was never the same. Listening to them discussing clothes reminded him of Patrick Jones describing the lone lady he had given directions to and he thought that he should speak to him again in relation to that incidence. Although there had been many hikers out that day there was not even one account of a lone lady having been seen. Being questioned again about this lady Patrick was not able to recall exactly what she had been wearing and as he had been so positive giving his original statement the DI could only think that he had made it all up on the spur of the moment. But why, he thought, Amelia had said that she had seen him speaking to a lady and not wanting her identity known had he given an incorrect description of her. Reminding him that making false statements in a murder investigation was a very serious offence he asked him once again for a description of the woman. Patrick, worried that he might suddenly become a suspect, told of the conversation he had with his friend in relation to the Badgers. He was sure that she would not have had anything to do with the murder and not knowing that Amelia had seen them thought he could keep her from learning about it. He said that he had given a correct description of what she was wearing but that she intended going to see the waterfall was untrue. She only lived a short distance away and was going to a wedding that day. She had only come to meet him as she had been told that some stray dogs were in the forest and she was worried that she could not go and protect the Badgers.

The DI insisted on him giving her name and address as he would have to verify this account of things and set his records straight. Before he left he advised Patrick that if he found out that he had misled him in any other way he would take a far more serious view of it and he could expect to end up in a cell. Calling on the lady he was asked in to her house and shown photos of Badgers which she seemed to devote her whole life looking after. His experience left him in no doubt as to the truth in Patrick's story.

CHAPTER TWENTY-EIGHT

Extra Effort In The Murder Enquiry

The morning following the adjournment by the super, everyone became more focused and determined to bring the case to a successful conclusion. The DI asked the uniform division to do a house-to-house enquiry and ascertain if any of the residents had been in the hills or knew anyone who had been on that particular weekend. Posters were placed in shop windows requesting information and everyone known to have been in the hills were interviewed again. Angela Winters and Joan Davis were finally seen at the station by the super and Michael Jones reported to the DI on Thursday afternoon. Although many new leads were established no progress was made during the week which made the DI reassess all the information he had. DS Tobin, who still felt there was a connection with the casino, was delighted when his friend William rang him and told him of another handbag being reported missing in the casino bar. William, with the co-operation of the bar manager, had searched thoroughly but found nothing. William wondered was it just a coincidence that on all three occasions of a bag going missing Denis Barker had a day off. One of William's friends told of seeing Denis with one of the group who met in the room upstairs and who had been drinking in the bar the night the bag went missing. The man was a regular and the staff knew him as Jim. He had been questioned along with other customers there that night but had denied seeing any handbag. That very afternoon Denis Barker was stopped for speeding and while interviewing him the Garda noticed a purse on the passenger seat which was identical to one reported missing earlier in the week. Calling for back up the Garda detained him and handed him over to DS Tobin. His car was driven back to the station and he was taken in a Garda car to be interviewed. The purse turned out to be his own and he denied all knowledge of the handbag, found in his boot, which proved to be the one stolen in the casino bar, without any contents. He was held in custody while a warrant to search his house was obtained. He lived with his parents who, without hesitation, showed the DS his room. What a surprise they got when, opening his wardrobe, they were confronted with a box full of handbags. None of them had any contents but on searching further they discovered car keys, bank cards, driving licences and an array of usual handbag contents. At this point they were hoping to find the identity of the corpse in the morgue and bagged everything before heading back to the station. Each bank card and driving licence was checked and the owners identified leaving none to tie in with the murder. Denis Barker was released on bail pending a future court appearance. He denied ever having a partner and said he stole all the bags himself. The super was convinced of Jim's involvement but was unable to act until the investigation at the casino by the international division was completed. Jim, on hearing of the search at Denis's house became nervous and worried Denis would reveal his name, cleared his boot and dumped everything into a skip which was in a garden close by. The house owner seeing him complained to the Gardai who sent a patrol car around to investigate. On seeing the contents that had been dumped they secured the area and waited for the forensic team to arrive. Among the contents dumped was a purse containing foreign bank cards and a foreign driving licence. The photo on the licence looked like the lady that had been murdered and the date of birth was consistent with their thoughts. Following a series of international phone calls it was believed that Lena Nowak had come for a holiday and her family had not seen her since. It was arranged for her brother to come over and if possible identify her. He broke down but with the aid of an interpreter he said that it was his sister. He could not understand why anyone in a foreign country where she was not known would want to murder her. Not having seen the registration of the car the house owner was unable to help them but among the fingerprints found on the bankcards one matched those of Jim Mescal, a petty thief, who was known to the Gardai. As this was part of a murder investigation a call to locate him was sent to all regions but Jim Mescal could not be found.

CHAPTER TWENTY-NINE

Analysing the Latest Information

The super, discussing the most recent events with her superiors, advised them of the matched fingerprints. It looked, at last, as if they could have a successful conclusion to this exasperating case. DS Tobin, having read all the previous notes on Jim Mescal, noted that up to that point in time he had only been regarded as a petty thief and wondered if he could actually commit a murder. If only they could discover where Lena Nowak had been in the days leading up to her death. Her brother remembering what he had been told to say, though an interpreter, had indicated that she had been in the country for about a week looking for her husband who had left her shortly after their wedding many years earlier but had no idea where she had been staying. Enquiries were made in all the local hotels and guest houses but it was not until photos were distributed that there was any reaction. A lady, the owner of a B & B said that she had stayed with her for two nights and said on leaving that she was going to a relative's house for a few days and would be back to collect her things before going home. She told DS Tobin that she was surprised when Denis Barker, the barman from the casino, came to pick her up. Jacks first thoughts were that now they could get the name of her relative and the address he had taken her to. He reported back to the DI who had different thoughts altogether. He was inclined to believe that

Denis could have committed the crime and given the handbag to Jim Mescal for disposal. Calling to the casino they learned Denis had a day off, so went out to his home which they knew from the day of the search. Finding out that he lived very close to the B&B that Lena Nowak had stayed in sent shock waves through Jacks body and he wondered if Denis had seen him calling to that house. Answering the door Denis invited them in and gave them the information they were looking for. Explaining that a customer in the bar, saying he was a relative, asked him to bring a lady to a house on the outskirts of the town close to where Mr Goode lived. He said that she asked to be left there and he returned to work. He had no idea where she went after that. The DI advised him not to leave the area as he would need to speak to him again very soon. He said nothing to him about Jim or the handbag that he had been observed dumping in the skip. Calling out to the address, which Denis had given them, it was obvious that it was not occupied so they went across the street and called on Mr Goode hoping that he could help them. He confirmed that the house had been unoccupied for years and said he had not seen anyone around it for a long time. "Were you thinking of buying it" he asked the DI. "We were led to believe that a lady had visited a relative there a short time ago and we are anxious to trace her." "The only lady here recently was the one dropped by that barman from the casino. She knocked here, enquiring about the same house, saying that she believed a relative lived there. Once she realised that it was unoccupied she said that she needed to return to town. As she had a suitcase with her I called a taxi and she headed back down the road." "Did you know the taxi driver" he asked Mr Goode. He answered the DI by saying "it was not a taxi but a customer from the casino who had been asked to pick me up and bring me to the post office but took the lady instead." "I need you to give me the number you rang and perhaps he will remember where he left her." "I do not remember that number as it was the lady who gave it to me to make the call." "Can you give me some idea of when this was." "It was a few weeks ago, I am sure it was a Friday as I remember thinking that I could have gone to collect my pension." "Would it have been before or after the night of the full moon." "Of that I am not sure but if you give me a minute I will check my pension book. You see, due to her calling, I missed going to the post office and had to collect a double week the following

Friday." Checking the dates in his book he told them that it was the Friday following the full moon. The DI gave Jack the task of requesting information relating to calls, made by Mr Goode, from the telephone provider. He had only made one call that day and it was to the casino. The security man, Kevin Burke, remembered receiving a call, for a taxi, from Mr Goode and at the time wondered if he had rung the wrong number. As he thought Mr Goode wished to collect his pension he asked one of the customers to collect him. He was just finishing his shift and had forgotten all about it until the DS had reminded him. "Do you remember who you asked?" "Oh yes it was a friend of Denis the barman, a man by the name of Jim Mescal." As soon as he heard this, alarm bells started to ring in his head so he rushed back to speak to the super and the DI. The super listened intently as the information unravelled and all three of them went over to see the previous postings on the notice board. They felt that things were finally coming together and they could reduce the number of prime suspects to a few. We need to speak to Denis Barker and certainly to Jim Mescal when we locate him. We need to go out again to Mr Goode and hopefully he will agree to officially identify Jim as the person who picked up Lena Nowak. Accompanied by two Gardai the DS was sent to pick Denis Barker up for questioning, and a nationwide alert was issued for Jim Mescal as the DI went out to have another chat with Mr Goode. Denis, thinking he was being quizzed about the handbags, came willingly to the station. In the interview room, when confronted with the murder enquiry, he denied knowing anything and said that he and Jim just took handbags for fun and believed that Jim could not kill anyone. He was adamant that every bag they took ended up in his house. He sounded very convincing but the super knew, from experience, that this may not be the case. Denis told her that he had not seen Jim for a week and had no idea where he might be. Reminding him that this was a murder enquiry the super told him how serious holding back information was and the consequences of it. Saying he understood all of that he promised to let them know if he learned anything new. Not having anything other than the stealing charge against him he was released and they reminded him not to travel without advising them. Jack was inclined to believe Denis and decided to look for information on Kevin Burke who looked after security at the casino. Searching through the Garda files he could not find any mention of him. He found this strange as usually to get a security position you had to be vetted and cleared and a record kept on the computer. Ringing the casino manager he learned that he had been given the job while still in the army and had been highly recommended by his CO. He was a very competent security guard and kept any undesirables from entering. Speaking to the CO he heard that he had served seven years in the army and had changed his name on becoming an Irish citizen. His original name was Alfonsi Nowak and he had resided in Ireland for ten years. Jack could not believe that he had the same family name as the deceased. This was too much of a coincidence for him, so he hastily gave the information to the DI who wondered how many of these possible suspects, all with a connection in the army, knew each other. There was Bert Delaney, injured in hospital, Colm O'Hara, the train waiter who was on leave, Jim Mescal still missing and Kevin Burke alias Alfonsi Nowak the security guard at the casino. As Kevin Burke was the only one available the DI decided to bring him in for questioning with the hope of gaining some new information that would help them with the investigation. The first question, he put to him, was an attempt to ascertain if he was related to the deceased. When asked he told the DI that many families, where he came from, had that family name but as far as he was aware he was not related. The DI was surprised at that answer and wondered how Kevin had known the name of the murdered lady. He decided not to ask him at that moment with the intention of throwing him off later. Asking him the whereabouts of Jim Mescal he was assured that he had not seen him for about a week. A half hour of questions and with nothing new emerging he asked him how he knew the name of the woman in the morgue. He said that he remembered that Bert Delaney had called in to see him following his visit to the morgue and knowing his previous name had asked if they were related. He told the DI that he would have known if a member of his family had been in Ireland so he was sure it was not one of them. Once again the DI did not believe him as they had not identified her at that time so it would not have been possible to see her name. Another piece of the puzzle that he must remember and put to good use, when required, in the future. Enquiring about Bert, Kevin told him that he was still in hospital unable to see anybody. He had gone to visit him but had been refused permission on the grounds that he was still in a coma. Coming close to the time limit for questioning he asked Kevin for details of the night that he had received the phone call from Mr Goode requesting a taxi. He said, he remembered that at the time, thinking Joe Goode wanted to collect his pension and to save him the cost of a taxi he had asked Jim Mescal to pick him up. Do you know if he did bring him to the post office? He lost no time in saying that this happened at the end of his shift and he had not seen him since. He told the DI that Jim was usually very reliable so he would assume that he had. "Do you recall what you did that evening after you finished work" the DI asked him. "That was the evening I tried to visit Bert in the hospital and afterwards I went for a few drinks with some friends." The DI watched him as he drove away and realised that, although the interview had lasted for two hours, he had not learned anything new. This was very unsettling and his instinct was leading him to believe that Kevin had been concealing something. Whether it had anything to do with the murder he did not know. Speaking to the super he asked her if it would be possible for her friend Leo to keep an eye on Kevin when he was at the casino. The super was surprised at this request and wondered if the DI knew of her relationship with Leo. Answering him she gave the impression the Leo was just a casual friend and could not impose on him to do something like that. Later that evening, as she was having a drink with Leo, she asked him how well he knew Kevin and was delighted when he told her that he did not know him at all. He agreed to observe him and see who his acquaintances were and if possible to learn something about him. Usually, following an evening together, Leo would call a taxi and leave Una home before heading to his own house. He was surprised when, on reaching her apartment, she asked him would he like a coffee before going home. Sensing that she wished to continue their earlier conversation he accepted her offer and accompanied her inside. Offering him a glass of wine it soon became apparent that she had other ideas for the rest of the evening. They had been seeing each other for six months but other than a good night kiss they had never expressed a desire to see their relationship change. He had often wondered what she was like as a woman instead of a Garda superintendent and it looked as if he was about to find out. The room was warm and cosy as they sipped their glass of bubbly and they both knew that tonight would start a new phase in the relationship. It was if a script had been written for them as they gently held each other close and felt the first tremors of excitement running through their bodies. Their kissing grew more intense as the explored each other's body. Somehow or other they shyly undressed each other and unconsciously made their way to the bedroom. Under the cool sheets they made uninhibited passionate love and wished it would go on for ever. Thoughts of going home never entered his head as they lay happily together and fell asleep in each other's arms. Waking up and realising it was Sunday they once again held each other close and enjoyed another few hours of utter bliss. Una finally got up with the intention of preparing something to eat but Leo convinced her that they should celebrate their new found love by going out for lunch. As they got themselves ready to go out they enjoyed a pot of tea and a slice of toast. He was like a schoolboy as they walked hand in hand along the street and thought to himself what a difference a day makes. Neither of them noticed the knowing smile on Jack Tobin's face as he made his way to the football match.

CHAPTER THIRTY

Last Meeting Before Amsterdam

On that same Saturday evening the 'charity group' volunteers met for their final meeting before handing their contributions over to their partners in Holland. Luke was in flamboyant mood as he thanked everyone for all the work they had done and congratulated them on the amount collected. They heard him say "As you all know Gareth will be flying to Amsterdam on Friday and will hand the cash over with the same degree of secrecy as we have here. We will get official recognition later on and a detailed account of what uses it will be put to. We will resume our fund-raising efforts in a few weeks' time so in the meantime take a well-earned rest until I contact you." Charlotte felt as if they were being dismissed without her learning anything new, so she tried to prolong the meeting by asking when would they find out the true value of their effort. Luke, unable to think of an answer, changed the subject and asked Gareth was he prepared for the trip. In reply, Gareth said that everything was organised and he was looking forward to his return trip, on Sunday, which as he loved sailing, would be by sea. Nobody, except Charlotte, paid much attention to this as all they wanted to do was finish the meeting and go home. The meeting broke up with much shaking of hands and friendly hugs, everyone promising to be back in a few weeks. Luke was furious as he watched Charlotte's reaction on hearing Gareth saying that he was returning by sea. He confided in Margaret but she had not noticed anything unusual and told him that he was over reacting. She suggested returning to the yacht to finalise their plans and knowing what this would lead to, he put Charlotte out of his mind, and agreed to go. Charlotte, as she reported her findings to the super, knew they would be helpful. Her thoughts, once more, turned to Jack as she hoped the weekend would see the end of Luke and the rest of the group and she could feel Jacks arms around her once again. Never having been in love before she was only beginning to understand the pain and the ecstasy that her friends spoke about. She would never have believed it possible for her to feel so much in love and so lonely without Jack, having only recently met him.

CHAPTER THIRTY-ONE

Waiting For Instructions

Luke and Margaret were still on the yacht and also unable to contact Jim. Margaret was thinking of how she could become a permanent feature in Luke's life while Luke was trying to work out how he would handle the collection on Sunday. He needed to be sure that Jim would be there with a fast car and could not understand why he was not answering his calls. He knew that Gareth would make the transition as simple and fast as possible. Lobster pots sounded a great idea as they could be left, untouched in position, without causing suspicion if there were people about. He had never lifted pots before and hoped special equipment would not be needed. Having spent the week on board with Margaret he was calm and relaxed and as they devised a scheme to take the delivery ashore he was looking forward to making a lot of money. He had not heard that Jim was in hiding and although not hearing from him he still believed that a car would be available. Margaret suggested leaving her Mercedes, out of sight, at the casino and use Jim's transport to convey the diamonds from the yacht to the casino where they could transfer everything later into her car for bringing to the cottage. She reasoned that if the shipment had been monitored then Jim, not them, would be picked up by the Gardai and although they might lose everything they would remain free to start again. Luke, knowing how logical Margaret was, agreed to do this and they began to put a timetable in place. Gareth had flown out that morning and they awaited his instructions regarding the pickup coordinates. They had told Jim to be in the casino, with the car, on Sunday when they would let him know his role in the final project. They believed that he had secured a car but would not get in touch with them until required. Mark was just a volunteer but to avoid him getting suspicious he was asked to be available in case he was needed and they expected him to be at the casino with Jim. Tina, Mary and Charlotte had all finished up the previous Wednesday. Unknown to any of the group Mark was an accomplice of Gareth's and knew more than anybody of the treachery going on. He was constantly cooperating with Gareth on their unfolding plan, which if it worked out, would turn all Luke's ideas upside down. He and Gareth had ambitions of their own and used Luke's charity cover to their own advantage. They had worked out that Charlotte was not what she claimed to be but as long as she concentrated on Luke they felt they had nothing to worry about. They would be long gone before anybody noticed. Luke, never having had reason not to trust them, continued to include them in his plans unaware of their intentions. Jim was not involved with them but was caught up in a different scenario and would not be there with a car when he was needed. He could not risk anybody finding out where he was hiding so did not answer any calls. Nervously waiting for the last stage of the operation to begin Luke and Margaret had a few drinks and fell into each other's arms. Love making was their favourite way of relieving stress and they playfully undressed each other before enjoying a warm scented bath together. Lying between the cool silk sheets, the aroma of Black Opium drifting across his nostrils, Luke's senses were reeling as his hands explored her soft white body. Margaret, always aware of his impetuous nature, restrained her movements until she too was ready for the beautiful explosion she knew they would experience. At that moment neither of them had a single thought, on anything, other than the magical sensations running through their bodies. It was moments like this that compensated for the worries and strife of their everyday living. Margaret remained lying between the sheets as Luke prepared the dinner. They remained on board the yacht overnight with the intentions of preparing for their delivery which they expected early Sunday morning. They spent some time looking up weather forecasts, wind conditions, tide timetables, coastal charts and lobster pot positioning along the coast. Happy that they were ready to follow Gareth's instructions when they received them they hoped to hear from him first thing in the morning.

CHAPTER THIRTY-TWO

Amsterdam

It was two weeks since Lena had been murdered and Gareth had finally come to believe that her death had nothing to do with their past. It had been a terrible shock to him and not having any idea who was responsible had been very distressing. Why had she been in the woods? She had not told anyone that she had arrived and he wondered why. Normally they would all get together and renew their pledge of silence so what was different this time? None of the comrades had mentioned seeing her and he wondered what her reason was for going so far into the forest. Had she come with somebody else this time and just went for a walk before being murdered? Knowing of her ongoing mental health issues he found it hard to believe that she would have trusted anybody unless she knew them really well. He hoped that it was not any of the comrades, who because she arrived unexpectedly, felt threatened and decided to do away with her. Today as he headed out to Holland he would have to remove all those thoughts out of his mind and concentrate on what he had to do. Had he known what forces were building up against him he would have thought differently.

Still at home, she he had not heard of Lena's murder and still thought that she had an alibi for what she was about do. A phone call alerted her to the fact that Gareth was heading for Amsterdam on

Saturday and that is to where she travelled with the intention of ensuring that she could follow him. She watched as he came out of the airport and observed the undercover police also watching him. Thinking that if she got too close she could get caught up in his arrest she held back and advised her contacts to keep an eye on things for her.

As he arrived in Amsterdam, Gareth was feeling nervous as he worried about being stopped by customs and would have no explanation for all the cash he was carrying. Passing through the airport without incident he was very relieved but had he known the reason for him not being stopped he may have thought differently. He had been monitored leaving the Irish airport and the details forwarded to the police in Holland. From the moment he stepped off the plane his every movement was carefully watched. If everything went to plan they would see the transaction taking place and could identify the local criminals. The plan was to allow everything to happen without interference and when they were happy that Gareth was on his way with the goods to arrest the gang while they still had the cash. They would follow Gareth and report whatever mode of transport he intended using and leave it up to the Gardai to take up the chase. Ten minutes after leaving the airport Gareth went into a bar and ordered a drink. Sitting at a table, his briefcase never leaving his side, he slowly sipped his beer. He was not aware of the undercover police watching him constantly. With clockwork precision he went into the toilets as a gentleman walked out. Nobody saw the exchange as briefcases were swopped and without losing a stride both men continued walking in opposite directions. Garret's briefcase containing the cash was out on the street and into a waiting car before Gareth had closed the inner toilet door. Gareth reappeared with a briefcase but this one contained pure diamonds. Finishing his beer he nonchalantly walked out of the bar and boarded a tram which took him close to the harbour.

The cars, carrying the police, followed it and watched as he made his way to a fishing boat moored along the quay wall. He climbed effortlessly on board to what looked like an empty trawler. They patiently waited for someone to arrive with the diamonds and were shocked when darkness fell and the boat silently moved out into the bay. Now believing that the exchange would take place at sea they sent for the coastguard launch to observe the transaction taking place. By the time the launch arrived Gareth, unseen, had transferred to a different vessel and was heading about ten miles upstream to a prearranged spot where he would take refuge overnight. The fishing boat sailed slowly out to sea followed by the launch and it soon became apparent that something had gone wrong and no transaction was going to take place. The fishing boat was escorted back to port where, to the dismay of the police, no sign of Gareth could be found. The crew denied ever seeing him and maintained that they were just fishermen going to the fishing grounds when they had been intercepted and ordered back to the harbour.

Her contacts like the police had lost track of him but told her they would find out where he was very quickly. They unlike the police had contacts everywhere and when something as big as a diamond heist had taken place everyone was on high alert. Information was bought and sold and very little went on without it being known.

Time was passing as Luke and Margaret waited to hear from Gareth. They began to get worried as the hours went by and wondered had he been apprehended in Amsterdam. As dawn broke Luke started his engine, let go the mooring ropes and headed out to sea, hoping to spot Gareth as he laid the lobster pots in place. Perhaps, he thought, Gareth was unable to communicate with him as he knew that his calls were being monitored and would just lay the pots as planned. Not having made definite arrangements he was unsure of the exact location but felt it would be along the stretch of water usually used by the lobster fishermen. Not wanting to attract attention, by staying in one area, he sailed slowly southwards along the coast watching out for any sign of Gareth. By noon he was convinced that Gareth had been apprehended and everything he had worked for was lost. He turned around and headed back alongside where he tied up once again. Margaret, in an attempt to relieve the tension, offered to take him up town and buy him a meal. He knew that he would need to keep calm if he was to have any success working out this problem and accepted her offer. They showered and dressed for the evening and calling a taxi made their way to the restaurant. While waiting for their meal Luke remembered that Jim would have been waiting for instructions at the casino and would have been wondering why he had not contacted him. Ringing Jim, and not being answered, left him troubled and he started to wonder could there be a connection between this and Gareth not getting in touch? He never thought that Gareth would have deceived him and held on to some hope that he would hear from him soon. Having a nice meal and a bottle of Saint Emilion relaxed him and returning to the yacht with Margaret he knew he would enjoy her company and get through the night. He would face his problems in the morning.

The Garda international division, with the assistance of the Dutch police, had spent many months working on this case and had high hopes of a successful outcome. Relationships with their police counterparts, in Holland, was exceptional and they knew that they also had a desire to put a stop to this particular group selling illegal diamonds to the highest bidder. Everything had been put in place to watch the yacht picking up the diamonds from the lobster pots and on their return to raid the casino and arrest Luke and the remaining group members who they expected to be there. The yacht had been followed as it sailed along the coast but there had been no attempt to go close to any of the lobster pots. After returning to the harbour he and his lady friend had been observed all evening in the restaurant but no activity had been noticed and following the meal they had returned to the yacht.

Early that day the police in Amsterdam had advised them that Gareth had landed that morning and was being shadowed but then they had heard nothing. It was as if all communications had been severed. As the hours passed they got increasingly concerned and wondered what could have gone wrong. Not wishing to intrude, on what might be turning out to be a difficult assignment, they refrained from picking up the phone. Finally they got a call from an embarrassed superintendent telling them they had lost Gareth. They believed that there had not been a hand over and would continue their search for him and the cash. This was a big disappointment for the Gardai after having such high expectations but they held on to a glimmer of hope that he would be found. They would continue to watch the casino and hopefully see Jim arriving there. If he was not taking in for questioning about the Diamonds they could hand him over to the DI who they knew were looking for him in connection with the murder.

On the other side of the channel Gareth was feeling very pleased with the way things had worked out. He had rested comfortably overnight in a 'safe house' where enjoying a glass of wine he had begun to look forward to his life in the sun. He had planned this charade for months and now he could relax and begin a new phase in his life. He had worked hard convincing Luke to allow him to collect the diamonds while behind the scene he had been organising his own piece of the action. On his previous visits he had befriended a couple who were trying to break into the big-time diamond trade and having promised them a share of the proceeds convinced them to work with him. Being local they were able to organise the escape boat and the safe house. They already had good contacts in the diamond trade and although the price was less than elsewhere it was a quick way of passing off the gems. Gareth received four hundred and fifty thousand American dollars and did not question how much the couple got. They had many contacts and he had been put on a fishing boat heading to England. On arrival he was handed a ferry ticket to Bilbao and it was to Spain that he travelled. He thought that not having committed a crime, other than stealing Luke's diamonds who could not report it, he would not be looked for by the police. At last he could turn his back on petty crime and live a decent life. He felt no sympathy for Luke and knew that he would just start off again on another fund-raising scam. He had used Mark to cover his tracks but the time had come to make a clean break from his past. All he could think of was that Mark never had any idea of what he had been planning and would never think of him being in Spain. It would be his time to sit back and relax and not worry what had gone on in his life in the past. Had he known that Mark, who was much brighter than he had given him credit for had guessed for some time what he had been planning, he may not have been so smug. Also unknown to him was the fact that Mark was part of an international gang with good connections and it would not be long before he found out where he was living. Neither did he know that her contacts had spotted him going on to the ferry and it was known that he was on his way to Bilbao. The following morning as there was still no sign of progress having been made in Amsterdam the Gardai maintained a watch on Luke and Margaret on board the yacht and hoped that they would eventually lead them to where Gareth was hiding.

The Superintendent recalled Charlotte and felt it would be safer for her to remain working in the office until a conclusion had been reached. Getting bored with the routine office work she went on the computer hoping to find some background information on either Luke or Jim. Jim as he was first alphabetically came up almost immediately and as she checked out his file she became aware of a link to his past. Somehow unnoticed, up to now, was a reference to his army career which showed that he had been discharged for attempting to sell guns and ammunition to a criminal gang. He had later secured a job as a courier in an unknown company that was run by a Luke Devine. She realised that she had never learned Luke's family name while working for the charity and was interested to establish if it one and the same person. She got no further with her enquiries as her superintendent called her to her office and advised her that she was being sent on a course that could lead to promotion in the future. Unofficially she told her that it was felt that she would be safer away from the station until Luke and his group were apprehended. She was disappointed but unable to refuse she headed to Templemore to take up the course.

Still under orders not to see Charlotte a very lonely Jack could only wait for things to change. Hearing her voice, as he lifted his phone, gave him a lift but this was short lived as she told him about the course. His thoughts were that she was being sent offside for her own safety. On the other hand he believed it would give them a chance of getting together away from prying eyes. Before hanging up she promised to get in touch once she had settled in. As he accepted that they would not see each other for a while he set about locating Jim Mescal but did not know where to start. He, like Charlotte, opened the computer looking for any background information he could find and could not believe it when he saw a reference to his army days. Seeing an unknown courier firm had employed him, following his departure from the army, arose his suspicions and he thought that it would be a good place to start his enquiries. Not having been involved with the casino investigation the name Luke Devine meant nothing to him. The address for this company was a PO number but when he rang the post office he learned it was a bogus number. Starting back at the beginning he paid a visit to the CO at the army barracks. Commandant Harris had only recently taken on this role and knew nothing of a Jim Mescal. Hearing that it was a murder investigation he advised Jack that he would go through the records and see if he could find anything that might help. On the off chance that Luke Devine's name may be linked somehow with Jim's he asked the CO to watch for it also. Never having had much luck in dealing with the forces he did not hold out much hope of receiving any information. Much to his surprise he received a call the following day asking him to call back to speak to the CO and was overwhelmed by the information he was given. Jim Mescal had been caught selling goods and was discharged. There was no record of a Luke Devine but he had been friendly with a Bert Delaney and Colm O'Hara. The CO believed that Bert Delaney was in the military hospital recovering from an accidental shooting and Colm O'Hara was working, as a waiter, on the trains. There was no mention of Kevin Burke but perhaps that was because his name was Alfonsi Nowak at that time. After thanking the CO for the valuable information he made his way back to the station. The DI was pleased that he could now tie the three names together but it did not help him to find Jim Mescal.

Jack's thoughts were now focused on hearing from Charlotte and although he continued his attempt to find Jim Mescal all he could think of was being with her again. The memories of her soft skin close to his and the scent of her perfume wafting across the bedroom took over and all he could visualise was the vision of the most beautiful girl he had ever seen. It had been a difficult time not being able to hold her close and he wondered if she felt the same way. His thoughts were interrupted by the super calling his name and asking how the search for Jim Mescal was proceeding. He was lost for words for a few moments as he had been dreaming of Charlotte and not concentrating on his work. The super told him that she had been impressed with the manner in which he had obtained the information regarding the three army buddies and wondered if Kevin Burke or anyone else had been involved with them. Kevin Burke was brought in again and denied all knowledge of knowing Colm O'Hara. They already knew of his association with Bert Delaney and Jim Mescal. He maintained that he only knew Jim Mescal from the casino and had never met him during his time in the army. After he left the station the DI and DS looked closely at the earlier statements and concluded that he had not told them the truth. Bert Delaney had known Jim Mescal, Colm O'Hara and Kevin Burke during their time in the army. Kevin had said that he did not know Colm and only knew Jim through the casino. As they had all served in the same regiment at the same time they found it hard to believe that they did not all know each other and wondered why they would deny it. Would it be that they all shared a secret from the past which they did not want anyone to know about. Jack was finding it more difficult, each day, to concentrate on his job as all he could think about was Charlotte. Oh how he longed to hold her close, to feel her soft skin close to his, to see that sparkle in her eyes and sense the excitement in her body. He could not understand why she had not rung him; he had believed that she had feelings for him but as time went by he was becoming disillusioned. If only she would ring and let him hear her voice, tell him where she was and hopefully arrange for them to meet. In his dream world he hardly noticed the super coming into his office and was caught completely off guard when she asked him how the investigation was going.

His computer was running with the case files open but as he had not been concentrating he had no way of knowing how things were. He knew there was no point in winging it so he just admitted to not being up to speed but promised to give her a report within the hour. Her appearance had shattered his thoughts on Charlotte and he settled down to see what he could deliver. There had not been any significant developments but as he looked through the most recent information he observed that a phone call had come in relating to a set of car keys that had been found in the woods close to the car park. He wondered if they could be the missing keys from Meg Walsh's car. Thinking about the woods he wondered if Jim had been hiding in the cottage where Charlotte had worked for a few days. Going back to the super with his limited report he asked her what she thought of the idea. Knowing the uncertain elements in the casino case she had to warn him off doing anything that might interfere with that investigation. Bringing up the subject of the keys she told him that they had been brought to the station by Anthony Gleeson the café owner who said that they had been handed in by a hiker. They were the missing keys and everyone connected with the case wondered had they been accidently dropped or just discarded. Jack who had his own suspicions surrounding the café was thinking that Anthony may have had them all along. Perhaps his early morning meeting with Amelia had more to it than imagined.

The end of another day and as Jack headed home his mind focused on Charlotte once again. He could not decide whether he was still under orders not to ring her but he so badly wanted to see her and hold her close that he was prepared to get in touch even if it was against orders. Twice he picked up the phone to ring her but each time remembered her telling him that she would ring him. He had been sure that he would have heard from her and now began to fear that she was under pressure herself and unable to do so. As he picked up the phone again it rang in his hand and he almost dropped it with the shock. Hearing from her was exciting and he could not disguise the joy in his voice. She too was thrilled to experience a wonderful, indescribable loving feeling as they finally got to speak to each other again. She had only rung to let him know that she was fine and that everything was going well but as they conversed she knew she needed him to join her for the weekend. They spoke for over an hour before arranging a secret rendezvous at the hotel where she was staying. They knew they could not be seen together but were determined to have a weekend with each other somehow. After they said goodnight Jack relaxed and began to look forward to them getting together. Tomorrow, he thought, he would make a list of all outstanding items that needed tiding up in the case and try to make some headway in locating Jim Mescal.

The day started by him going through things with the DI during which time they realised that there were still a number of questions that needed answering. Opening a new page they began to think aloud and make notes. Was Amelia Jones and Anthony Gleeson's meetings purely romantic or had they some other reason for being out so early in the morning? Would Pauline Smith and her husband have had a walk in the hills that day as her motorbike was out of action? Who was Declan O'Grady meeting when he went out after six-thirty that evening? They had still not been advised on Bert Delaney's condition and thought it would be prudent to get back in touch with his CO. They needed to interview him in connection with his wife's abduction and his knowledge regarding the body in the morgue. Colm O'Hara had returned back from his trip to New Zealand and his version of events might open up new avenues to be investigated. Jack recalled taking the car registration when he had seen somebody pick up a man off the yacht but with all that was going on he had not checked it out. This would need to be done right away. The DI made a note to interview Stephen Cloak again and that only left them looking for Jim Mescal. Thinking of Jim reminded them of Denis Barker and they wondered if any of the casino group could have been involved with the murder. Due to the ongoing international investigation they were unable to interview any of the suspects but now thought that Denis may be able to give them some of their names. It was a long shot but they felt, if they went about it the right way, they might get some valuable information from him. They were just beginning to make a start on their list when the super came in with new information regarding Kevin Burke.

She had been told that he had given in his notice and was returning to his homeland. She had taken it up with the legal department and had been advised that unless there was reason to believe that he was involved in a crime they would not have the power to prevent him leaving. They postponed their proposed action and concentrated on finding as much information as possible on Kevin Burke. They returned to the casino giving the impression that they were looking for Denis Barker and while Jack spoke to him the DI had a conversation with the manager. He confirmed that Kevin had given in his notice and would be leaving by the end of the week. The manager also told him that Kevin had a day off and had gone to visit a friend in hospital. Without a search warrant he could not demand to see where Keven stayed but as if reading his mind the manager asked him if he would like to have a look at the room. The DI guessed that he had his own reason for looking into the room but was glad to accept the offer. A quick look and it became obvious that most things were already packed and the DI wondered if he planned to leave before his notice expired. A waiter's jacket was hanging in the wardrobe and this puzzled the DI. Asking the manager had Kevin also worked as a waiter he got a definite no for an answer but he was able to point out a hotel crest on the jacket indicating that it belonged to the hotel opposite the casino. Somewhere in the back of his mind the DI recalled Lucy Delaney telling him of being bundled into a car by a waiter. He thanked the manager telling him not to disclose that they had been in the room. This suited the manager and he readily agreed. Going across to the hotel he asked Lucy if she would recognise the waiter who had abducted her. She said that it had been dark and she got such a fright she was afraid to look at him too closely but if you find the waiters jacket that he was wearing you will see that there is a button missing on the left sleeve which came off in my hand as he shoved me into the car. Getting up she went to her handbag and produced the button. Back at the station the DI explained what had occurred and the super felt that is was sufficient evidence to obtain a search warrant. As it was a murder investigation she was able to provide the DI with the necessary papers. The following morning armed with the warrant and supported by four Gardai he called on Kevin Burke and requested admission to his room. Kevin, thinking they were investigating the murder, got very agitated and had they not had a warrant would certainly have refused their request. He asked the DI what they were searching for and was annoyed when he was told they were looking for evidence but not for anything specific. The DI, spotting the waiters jacket, asked him if it was his and not thinking for a minute that it was what they were looking for told them that he had bought it as he had thought of working as a waiter before he got the security job. Inspecting the sleeve it was immediately apparent that a button was missing and on comparing the one he had been given he obtained a match. Bagging the jacket the DI said, "Mr Burke I would like you to accompany us to the station and answer some questions regarding the kidnapping of Lucy Delaney from the hotel across the road." Kevin could not believe that this had happened and found it hard to understand how they knew about the jacket or where they had obtained the button. He protested his innocence and denied all knowledge of the abduction. Down at the station he was questioned by the super and the DI for many hours but continued to say he knew nothing of the kidnapping. As he grew tired and frustrated the DI threw him off balance by asking him how he knew the name of the deceased lady in the morgue. He could not understand why the conversation had suddenly gone from a kidnap to a murder investigation. His mind was trying to work out how to reply without implicating himself when the DI shocked him further by asking was he the victim's husband and had he been involved in her murder. Before he had time to reply the superintendent reminded him that he shared the same family name as her and that she had come to Ireland looking for her husband. "How did you know her name" the DI asked him again? "Did you recognise her when Jim Mescal picked her up at Joe Goodes cottage or had you already seen her in the B & B close to where Denis Barker lives?" All these questions being thrown at him without giving him a chance to reply totally unsettled him and he could not think what to say. At this point he believed if he owned up to the kidnapping the relentless questioning would stop and he would have time to think things through. He was on the verge of confessing when he was advised that the session had come to an end and he could relax for two hours. The DI never knew how close he had been to closing that part of the investigation.

CHAPTER THIRTY-THREE

Jim In Custody

Jim, from where he was hiding at a friend's house, had a clear view of the harbour. He had watched as Luke sailed out and wondered how he would react when he returned and realised that there was no escape car standing by. He had no way of knowing what had happened but not wanting to be picked up in relation to the handbag stealing he was unable to make contact with anyone to find out. His part of the operation was to provide a car and as he had failed to do that he did not expect to get a share of the loot. He was much more concerned with the handbag contents he had disposed of and hoped Denis had been truthful with him as to where the bag had come from. Why had there been a wide search for him if it was only to do with a missing handbag. He decided to ring Denis and see if he knew what was going on. Denis, unaware of the skip incident, told him that the Gardai wish to speak to him in connection with the lady that he had picked up at Joe Good's house. He asked Jim did he remember where he had left her and advised him to go to the station and clear up the confusion. Jim was relieved at this information as he knew exactly where he had left her. He asked Denis if it had anything to do with the handbags to which he was assured it had not. Denis did not tell him about the search at his house and Jim, though aware of the house search, never mentioned dumping the handbag in the skip. His friend dropped him at the Garda station and he calmly walked in to speak to the DI. Nobody was more surprised than the DI and in the company of the super he escorted him to the interview room. They left him sitting alone as they checked the information they had collected. They had been advised that it was him who had picked up the woman from Mr Goode's house. They had his fingerprints on a credit card, belonging to the deceased woman, which had been found in the skip. Denis had implicated him in the stealing of handbags and with their knowledge that he was a friend of Kevin Burke wondered if he had a part in the kidnapping. Letting him speak first they learned he had come into the station to explain where he had left the lady that he had collected at Mr Goode's house. He said while coming in voluntarily he had not expected to end up being brought to the interview room and cautioned. At that moment he saw Kevin Burke as he was being brought to a cell to await his next interview. He pretended not to notice but both the super and DI saw his reaction and knew he had seen and recognised him. Once again they went out of the room and agreed that after they learned where he had left the woman they would speak to him about the kidnapping before mentioning the fingerprints on the credit card. "Now Mr Mescal" he heard the DI say before he was asked for the location where he had left the lady. He was still a little shaken after having seen Kevin Burke and was unsure whether he should continue to say anything. He was desperately trying to figure out if both of them were being questioned about the same woman or was there something that Denis had not told him. Knowing where he had left her now had him worried but believing he would be safer telling the truth gave them the address. He got a little agitated when he was asked who had instructed him to leave her there and replied that it was her wish to be taken to the café. He was unprepared for the next question and did not answer right away, when asked who had met her there. After a moment's hesitation he said she had gone in alone and he had driven home. They both wondered why, when being interviewed, Anthony Gleeson had not told them that a lady with a suitcase had been left at the café but decided that they would deal with that later. Jim sensed that there was more to this interview than he had imagined and telling them that he had told them everything he knew, asked if he could leave. He was devastated when they said that there were a number of outstanding items that they wished him to help them with. He could not believe that they had connected him with the kidnapping and on being questioned immediately denied all knowledge of it. As he sat there in front of the super and DI he remembered seeing Kevin Burke and began to panic a little. Part of him was convinced that Kevin would not have admitted to knowing about the affair but if he had not said anything how did they come to the conclusion that he was involved. He tried to think of what it was that triggered their interest in him. He had made sure the car had no fingerprints by wearing gloves and he was sure that Lucy would not be able to identify him. He had no way of knowing if Denis Barker had been involved, nor if he had, would he have spoken to the DI about it. He watched the super and DI closely and tried to read their body language but neither had given anything away. He thought they could be bluffing and decided to say no more. The DI, aware of the silence, reminded him of the seriousness of the crime and left him, once again, on his own to think things through. On his own he had lost some of his confidence and wondered should he have said that he had driven the car on the night of the kidnapping. He had just made up his mind what to do when Kevin Burke, as he passed the interview room, raised a clenched fist in his direction. He did not know what to make of it but was aware of it not being a good sign. Had they told Kevin that he had admitted to something or had it been a warning to him not to say a word. As they returned to the room, the super on opening her note book addressed Jim and said, "we have reason to believe, that not only were you involved with the kidnapping of Lucy Delaney, but with a far more serious crime, murder." He had never understood why all the fuss had been created over picking up a lady and bringing her to the café. That they had believed he was somehow involved in the kidnapping he accepted but had continued to deny any involvement. Murder was on a different scale altogether but he had not worried on that score as he knew that he had nothing to do with it and so they could not have any evidence to tie him to it. He relaxed a little and was confident that he would not have to admit to having any knowledge of the kidnapping as, at that point, he felt they were only clutching at straws. What a shock he got when the DI cautioned him and advised him that they were holding him for questioning in connection with the murder of Lena Nowak. He told them that as he had never met anyone by that name they could not have picked up any evidence to associate him with her or her murder. The DI stunned him when he said that they had found his fingerprints on an item belonging to that person. The DI concluded the interview having advised Jim that they would continue when he was prepared to tell the truth. As he was being taken to a cell he demanded that his solicitor be present at their next interview. There had been no sign of Kevin Burke but he overheard the super mentioning his name and believed that he was also being held for questioning. As they arrived back at the incident room, following the interview, DS Tobin told the super that Charlotte had been asked to meet Mark, a member of the fund-raising group, who she believed had no connection with Luke but who, she felt, had a close link with Gareth. He explained that her superintendent had been disappointed when Gareth had eluded the Dutch police and thought that any clue to his whereabouts would be welcome. She arranged protection for Charlotte even though it was unlikely that it would be necessary. Charlotte was apprehensive as she had never actually met Mark outside the charity group meetings and wondered how he had her number and why he had contacted her. The meeting had been arranged in an outdoor setting so that she would be in full sight of the undercover Gardai. On arrival Mark left her in no doubt as to his position, telling her that he had always been aware that she was a special friend of Gareth's and hoped she could help locate him. She was amazed as he said, "you may not have realised that Gareth and myself were good friends and I'd hoped that you could give me some idea of his whereabouts." He told her that he was not involved in anything underhand but that they had arranged to meet on his return from Holland and as he had not contacted him he was anxious for his safety. Charlotte was under no illusion regarding his pedigree and was glad to have security around her. She reminded him, that up to now, the only contact they had shared was the charity group and even if she knew where Gareth was, she would not be in a position to tell him. Before he thought of meeting her he had considered the possibility that she might not have known where Gareth was but decided to take a chance hoping it would save him some time. As he left he gave her his number and asked her to contact him if she had any news. He never mentioned knowing she was a Garda or that he had been aware of the security around the meeting. On the other hand he did not seem to realise that the Gardai, knowing that he was interested in finding Gareth, would follow his progress as he tried to locate him. With the knowledge that Gareth was a friend of Jim's and was also wanted in connection with the murder enquiry Charlotte's super had shared the information with DI Browne. He spent the next few hours, with DS Tobin and the super, analysing the information but had not reached a satisfactory conclusion. It was hoped that their interviews with Jim and Kevin would be more productive. Jack could not wait for the meeting to end so that he could travel to the hotel and be with Charlotte. Jack and Charlotte both realized that their getting together was going against orders and fraught with danger. He left his car in the high-rise carpark and took a taxi to the shopping mall close to Charlotte's hotel. He had not expected to find her being protected and was surprised when it was obvious that she was. He rang her phone telling her he had arrived and advising her of the Garda presence. He went to the bar and waited for the end of their shift. As the relief Garda was being briefed he took the lift to the top floor and walked back down to the third floor where Charlotte let him in to her room. The Garda had watched the lift but as it went up to the top floor he dismissed it as not being a threat to Charlotte. They waited to see if he had been observed but as the minutes ticked by they both relaxed and held each other tightly. Sitting close together on the settee they shared a three-course meal accompanied by a bottle of Merlot which she had delivered to her room. That was the moment they had hoped for, waited for, longed for. That was the moment when they knew that the waiting, although not by choice, had been worthwhile. It was the moment that they experienced that feeling of total togetherness that only two people in love can feel. Totally consumed with passion, their hearts thumping, their minds filled with excitement, they had enjoyed the luxury of the king-sized hotel bed as they sought to express their love for each other. How thrilling the weekend had been, how they had enjoyed each other and the excitement was added to by knowing that they should not even have been together. The on-duty Garda had rung her room when he had not seen her going down for breakfast and worried for her safety. Jack could not help but laugh when he heard her say she had enough to last her a week. Charlotte had not realised what she had said but also had a good laugh when Jack told her why he was laughing. Their time together had come to an end but they had already made plans to meet again. Charlotte left the room and as she headed back towards the college the Garda left the hotel and unobserved followed her to the car. Jack seized this opportunity and took a taxi back to where he had left his car. He had driven home conscious of the work he would need to catch up on following his weekend away but was unable to get thoughts of Charlotte out of his head. He had never experienced anything like this before and hoped it would last for ever.

The following morning at the station, just before the interview was due to begin, Jim had explained to his solicitor about leaving the lady to the café and confided in him regarding the kidnapping. He denied all knowledge of the murder and said that he did not believe that they could have his fingerprints on any item belonging to the murdered person. Jim did not realise that the lady in question, who he had picked up and left at the café, was the person who had been murdered. Neither did he know that the handbag and contents that he had placed in the skip belonged to her. His solicitor, knowing that he had already explained to the DI about picking up the lady and believing that he was not involved in the murder, advised him to own up to the kidnapping. He explained, to Jim, that on a kidnapping charge he could apply for bail and as he considered that there was no evidence relating to the murder charge he was confident that he would be released. Jim had not told him everything and when, during the interview with the DI, Jim went through the sequence of events relating to the kidnapping and he learned that he had slept in the car park, in the time frame of the murder, he was really taken aback. He requested an adjournment so as to speak to Jim. The super and DI were happy to grant an hour break as they needed to consider what they had heard and hoped that Jack had found something that they could put to use. On arriving back following his weekend with Charlotte, Jack had been handed a transcript of the interviews held with the two suspects. The DI instructed him to go through them as fast as possible and check them against the knowledge they already had. He reminded Jack that they would only have a few days to question them unless new evidence was secured and they would not be in a position to stop Kevin Burke from leaving the country. Jack convinced that Denis Barker was involved decided to call on him and question him in relation to the handbag that had been found in the skip. He bluffed, a little, as he pre-empted his interview by telling Denis that both Kevin and Jim were still detained and advised him to think carefully before he answered any of his questions. Denis wondered what, if anything, had either of them revealed. He was not sure what the DS was looking for and said nothing until asked a direct question. Being asked about the handbag in the skip he honestly answered that he knew nothing about it. The DS then said, "evidence on it may incriminate you so if you remember giving a handbag or knowing who gave it you would be advised to tell me now. Was there one bag perhaps that did not get to your house?" He felt that this line of questioning was for something bigger than theft and knowing the other two were being held he assumed it had to do with the kidnapping. That it may have to do with the murder never crossed his mind. His thoughts were focused on Kevin and Jim and their involvement in the kidnapping. He told Jack that Jim had been the driver and that Kevin had dressed up as a waiter. He had not heard of a handbag being taken but he understood that Kevin had gone to the carpark early on Monday morning to make sure that there were no fingerprints left on the car. His lady friend, who was somehow involved, accompanied him. Then Jack asked Denis who the lady was and where did she live. Denis was unable to give him that information as he did not know it himself. He was definite that he had not given Jim a handbag as any bags they came across went to his house. Jack had gone back to the station just in time to pass on the information before the interview was due to restart. That they could now tie both Kevin and Jim to the kidnapping and with the knowledge that they were both in the forest in the time frame of the murder made it a lot easier to conduct the interview. Jim's solicitor started the proceedings by asking for Jim to be released as he had explained the circumstances surrounding the lady he had picked up and had admitted to his part in the kidnapping. His attitude was that nothing more could be gained by holding him any longer as he had no further information to give. The super then threw a spanner in the works by asking Jim how his fingerprints were found on a credit card belonging to the deceased lady. Not knowing that the bag he had rummaged through, which had been given to him to dispose of and which he had put in the skip, belonged to the murdered lady he denied all knowledge of it and told his solicitor that he was being framed. A copy of the print and Jim's set of prints were presented to the solicitor and he had to agree that they were a match. At that point, the DI asked Jim when was the last time that he and Denis Barker had stolen a handbag or more to the point where did he dispose of the last bag he had handled? Jim was finding it difficult to listen to issues that he believed had nothing to do with him. He said that any bag they had stolen went to Denis Barker. The super then asked him did he remember where he got the bag that he took out of his boot and dumped? She was careful not to mention the site waiting for him to confirm where it was. Remembering what he had done and now believing that he must have been seen he told them that he had disposed of a bag in a skip as a favour for a friend. His solicitor once again asked for time to speak to his client but the super declined his request as she needed to make the most of her advantage and find out who his friend had been. Unwilling to give this information Jim was advised that he was being arrested on suspicion of the murder of Lena Nowak. His solicitor told him that bail could not be granted in a murder case without going to the high court but he would make an application as soon as possible. Jim was devastated and continued to plead his innocence as he was brought to a cell for the night. The DI was somewhat disappointed at the outcome as for some reason he felt that Jim was not the murderer. He had no evidence, other than the kidnapping charge, to hold Kevin Burke and reluctantly let him out on bail. He confiscated his passport and advised him to visit the station daily. He only had Denis Barkers word that he had been in the car park and knew that would not hold up in court. He notified immigration giving them both his original and changed names and advised them that he was not allowed to leave the country under any circumstances. Settling down in his office, after the trauma of the day, the DI met with Jack and examined the updated information that they now had. Jack thought they should check the café and see if anybody remembered a lady, with a suitcase, being left there by Jim Mescal. Neither Anthony nor Betty had any recollection of Jim leaving anyone there but as they left, a customer indicated that he would like to help them. Going outside he said that Anthony had not told the truth as he had seen them bringing a lady into their living quarters behind the café. He mumbled something about going back to finish his tea and he was gone before they had time to ask him his name. They wondered why they had denied seeing her but with only a stranger's word of the occurrence they thought it better to see how things developed before asking again. As they got back to their car Jack decided to return and get the strangers details. He was nowhere to be seen and his half cup of tea was still on the table. Anthony said that he did not know who he was, had never seen him before and thought he had left with them. There was only one door into the café and Jack felt that had he come back out he would have seen him. He asked Anthony to check the toilets but there was no sign of him there. Jack deduced that he must have been brought in through the same door as he had said Lena had gone and wondered was there more to Anthony Gleeson than they thought. He was now of the opinion that the suitcase was still in the house. He suggested having the café watched but the DI was not interested and they drove back to the station. While they were out a call had come in to advise them that Bert Delaney had regained consciousness but had no recollection of anything prior to the shooting. He did not remember his name or that he had been married and had no idea what a kidnapping was. The CO said that he would arrange a visit but the DI felt it would be a waste of time if he had no memory and would not be able to help him. The super advised him to take up the offer and judge the situation for himself. She reminded him that they had met in the morgue and he would notice any major change in Bert's attitude and demeanour. Arrangements were finalised but before he could go he thought it prudent to revisit all the information available and ensure that nothing had been overlooked. With Jack's assistance he put together the latest pieces of evidence and the names of those he considered still in the frame for committing the murder. He had Jim's fingerprints on the credit card but for some reason he did not believe that he was the culprit. Jim, he knew, was a member of the casino group that had been under surveillance and that put him thinking that there might be a connection to somebody involved with him there. Kevin Burke was guilty of kidnapping but if he was somehow caught up in the murder there was nothing to tie him to the case. It would be critical to discover who he was related to before he changed his name. It seemed too much of a coincidence that he and the deceased shared the same family name. Denis Barker was just a petty thief but it was always possible that something had gone terribly wrong with a bag snatch which led to the lady losing her life. The name of Colm O'Hara appeared on the screen and they realised that he had still not been interviewed. That would have to be given priority and done as quickly as possible. Perhaps he could open up new avenues to explore. Jack pointed out that all those on the list, with the exception of Denis Barker, had an army background and remind the DI that Anthony Gleeson had also served with the armed forces. He could not fit Stephen Cloak into the puzzle yet thought that he could have information helpful to the investigation. He was undecided as to whether he should still be considering Patrick or Amelia Jones, Michael Jones, members of the fancy-dress party, or the hike group. Was there a chance that some members of the birdwatchers may have been in the forest at that time? Who were the couple that Joe Goode had seen going towards the carpark early that Monday morning? Would that have been Kevin and his lady friend and if so could they be involved? They had identified the lone lady reported by Patrick Jones but wondered could the murder, be in any way, connected to the casino? He could not rule out the possibility that the murder had nothing to do with any of the suspects and had been committed by someone yet unknown. His going to visit Bert Delaney in the hospital was purely in connection with the kidnapping and yet, as he thought about it, he realised that Bert could have been in the woods after leaving Lucy in the cottage. This started a train of thought that led him to wonder had the shooting actually been an accident or an act of revenge by somebody close to the murdered woman. As he drove towards the hospital the DI rang Jack and asked him to return to commandant Harris and get a list of those involved with the training at the time of the accident. If the person who had fired the shot could be identified so much the better. Jack was at a loss to understand this new approach but believed that the DI had learned something new at the hospital. Arriving at the hospital at his appointed time the DI was escorted to a private room where Bert Delaney was sitting in a wheelchair. His escort, two MPs, positioned themselves in the room and advised the DI that they would be remaining for the duration of the interview. The DI was shocked at seeing Bert's physical condition and found it hard to compare him with the man he had dealt with at the morgue. Having been advised of his memory loss he had expected to be met with a totally different type of scenario and had not considered seeing such a physical deterioration. He had prepared himself for believing or disbelieving the loss of memory but now did not even know where to start. He introduced himself and was fully convinced that Bert had no idea who he was or why he was there. He asked Bert if he could tell him the time and although he was wearing a watch all he got was a blank stare. Reminding him again that he was a Garda and there to enquire about his involvement in the kidnapping he was asked what a kidnapping was. Thinking that he should never have gone to the hospital the DI, turning to the escort, indicated that he was finished and saying goodbye to Bert he walked out into the fresh air. He was escorted, without a word, to the hospital gate and was very relieved to get into his car and drive back to the station. His thoughts returned to the possibility of Bert's involvement in the murder and he wondered if there was a connection between it and the subsequent shooting accident. If he had not committed the crime could he have been in the forest at that time and witnessed it? Would he have known the assailant and was he part of a cover up? Knowing that Kevin Burke and Jim Mescal were involved with the abduction he considered it likely that Bert could also have been in the woods that day. Other than their army background he did not have any evidence showing a connection which would tie them together, yet somehow he felt that they were not telling him the truth when denying knowing each other during their army careers. He could not help thinking that Kevin Burke alias Alfonsi Nowak was somehow connected to the victim and decided to delve further into his background. He learned that before she was married Lena's Family name was Gorski and her cousin Jakub, while serving with the United Nations Peacekeeping Force, met Alfonsi Nowak who introduced her to his cousin Antoni Nowak. They got married but he disappeared soon afterwards and had not been heard of since. Arriving back at the Garda station the DI met Jack as he was leaving to meet Commandant Harris and took the opportunity to go with him. According to the records the accident involving Bert, took place during a training session being conducted for recruits preparing to join a United Nations Group and a sergeant from that unit was in charge. As the bullet had not been recovered it was impossible to say who had fired the shot that injured Bert Delaney. The Commandant was unable to confirm the visiting sergeants name but said the information could be released if a link to the murder could be proved. He told the DI that the group would be going overseas in about three weeks and it would be difficult to contact them for about five months after that. Leaving the camp the DI felt that the CO would have liked to have given him more information and was now convinced more than ever of a connection with the murder. He grew more determined to discover who it was that was being sheltered and to learn how many were involved in the cover up. Back at the station, as he was reminded that Jim Mescal was still being held, another set of thoughts started running through his head and he wondered did any of the casino group share army backgrounds or army connections. Knowing that Charlotte had been involved with the group he requested permission to allow Jack to visit her with the objective of gaining information which could help piece things together. Jack could not believe his luck as he headed officially to meet up with Charlotte and he hoped that they could make the most of their time together. He was bitterly disappointed as it emerged that their meeting would be conducted in a Garda station with little chance of them getting close together. The closest they got was sitting in front of a computer pulling out facts and figures. Charlotte thought that Mark had probably been in the army but as they checked his background it seemed more likely that he had been involved with criminal gangs. The Gardai, still looking for Gareth had been keeping Mark under observation and his file was right up to date. His last sighting had been, two days earlier, when he boarded a flight for Spain. The Spanish Police had been notified and asked to keep him under observation and try to find out who he was meeting. Charlotte, more interested in finding Gareth's whereabouts, honed in on this information and left Jack working on his own looking for what needed. She learned that Mark, on reaching Bilbao, went to the Hotel Gran and checked in before meeting his contact who he believed could lead him to Gareth. Jose was a member of the local drug trafficking gang and had a number of past dealings with Mark. He did not know the reason for Mark wishing to find Gareth but as he was being well paid for the information he did not care. He had already been paid for the same information by another interested person and could not believe all the interest in Gareth. Seeing them sitting together in the foyer drinking latte nobody would have guessed what they were up to. Neither of them were aware of the police observers watching their every move. Jose gave the required information and left quietly without telling Mark that others were also looking for Gareth or that he had already advised Gareth of his arrival. Gareth had been shocked to think that Mark could have found him so quickly and without a minute's notice left the apartment and took a train to Madrid. He booked into Hotel Nuevo as he waited to get a new apartment which would give him time to plan his next move. He took no notice of a lady following him on to the train and watching him as he went into the hotel. He wondered if Marks appearance in Spain meant that Luke also knew where he was and if so what consequences would it have for him? He began to realize that Mark could be a dangerous enemy and he needed to work out how best to deal with him. Knowing that he had abandoned him it would be necessary to come up with a good solution if he was to avoid a serious confrontation. His best option would have been to get in touch with him and invite him to share the profits from the sale of the diamonds but he did not want to lose any of his cash so felt he needed to come up with a better idea. Not wishing to spend the rest of his life running from him he thought about having him eliminated. Thinking it through he realised that would cost more than sharing and he would have a murder to answer for. Finally he decided it would be prudent to call him and renew their friendship and include him in his plans for the future. Mark, on receiving the call from Gareth explaining that it had not been possible to contact him and asking him to join him in Spain, knew that he had been forewarned and it would be a waste of time going to the address that Jose had given him. He did not tell Gareth that he was in Spain but carried on the conversation as if he was still at home. Gareth told him that he was in the process of moving to a new apartment and would give him the address in a couple of days. Mark returned to the airport and flew home without knowing that his movements had been watched all day. Charlotte suddenly realised that she had gone off on a tangent when she was supposed to be assisting Jack with his enquiries. She had not learned anything new and was unable to give him any information and she had never heard them saying anything that would have led her to believe that they had an army background. They remained together for as long as they felt possible and with a promise of returning soon Jack drove home.

 It was quite by chance that Luke and Margaret, who were spending a week in Madrid, saw Gareth as he booked into the very hotel that they were staying at. They were there to celebrate their engagement without any thought of Gareth or Jim who they had not heard from since the trip to Amsterdam. They decided not to ruin the first night of their holiday together and agreed to approach Gareth the following morning. Had they known the forces of evil already heading his way they may have thought differently. Later that evening, as he was sitting quietly in the bar, they observed a woman whispering something in his ear and taking his hand in hers led him towards his room. He could not believe that here in Madrid somebody could know what he had done in Amsterdam. How did she recognise him? Was it pure coincidence that she was in that hotel? What was she expecting from him? Had she approached any of his comrades? Going into the room she gave the impression that she wanted them to make love but as he moved towards her he felt the cold steel blade piercing his chest. His body slowly slid to the floor as she extracted the knife, placed it at his side and left the room. It was a clinical, efficient well practiced movement performed by an expert. She had earlier removed his briefcase taking every dollar he had possessed. A flight within the hour took her far away before his body was discovered the following morning. News of the murder was flashed across every channel bringing dismay to Luke as he feared that he might be associated with his death. Fortunately, Margaret and himself, following their meal, had stayed very late in the bar discussing how they would handle their meeting with Gareth and were seen to be there on CCTV. Luke, totally unaware of Gareth's background, felt that it was the money that had attracted the killer and thought that he would be still alive had he delivered the diamonds back to him. The lady going over to speak to Gareth was also seen on the camera but could not be identified or traced. Panic would be the only word to describe the feelings of the comrades as they digested the news of this latest killing involving one of their own. Had Lena not been killed nor Bert badly injured they would have put it down to an unfortunate incident and accepted it. Not knowing who was carrying out this vendetta against them they were terrified. Who could be so callous as to murder like that in cold blood? Worse still who was going to be next? If it was to do with their action all those years ago why had it not happened before now? Who could possibly have known and not taken action earlier? Kevin thinking back to that fateful day all those years ago tried to picture who had been involved. Finding it difficult to piece things together he went around to the newsagents to speak with Declan and Marge. With Jim still in custody, Bert in hospital and Colm working there were only the three of them to attempt finding a solution. They knew it had been a terrible accident but at the time panicked and did not know what to do. Disposing of Tobias's body instead of reporting the incident was unjustifiable and having to carry the guilt for so long intolerable. At the time Lena could not believe that her brother had been killed but as she was also firing her gun and it was not possible to establish whose bullet killed him she, like the others, had to remain silent. His commanding officer, having listened to him complaining for a long time, believed him to be absent without leave and although he placed him on the deserters list had never bothered looking for him. Lena's parents were both dead so there had been no one else to miss him. As far as Kevin was aware there was only the small band of comrades who knew what had happened and they were all sworn to silence. Shortly afterwards Lena agreed to marry Antoni and the celebrations were used to distract friends from thinking of where he could have gone to. Both of them knew that they would not stay together but it seemed a good idea at the time. Talking now to Declan and Marge, as they tried to recall what had transpired, they were filled with emotion and found the memories very difficult to handle. On that morning, the nine of them had gone out hunting as they had on many previous occasions. Usually there were ten in the group but Gretta was not well and could not go out with them. That left Lena, Tobias, Kevin (Alfonsi), Bert, Colm, Declan, Marge, Gareth and Jim. Now things were very different, of the eight who shared the secret there was Lena lying in the morgue, Gareth dead in Spain and Bert seriously injured in hospital. They were forced to think that it all had to do with their past as they considered what they could do to avoid any further bloodshed. Declan being a logical type of person asked them to look at a different scenario which switched their thoughts from the comrades to individual incidents. He thought that Lena had been murdered without any connection to the past and Bert's injury was the result of an unfortunate accident. Gareth, who they knew had absconded to Spain with Luke's diamonds, had been killed for the money and had nothing to do with them. As they were unable to think of anybody, who might have learned of their deception, doing something so horrific as this, they hoped he was right and calmed down a little. In the Garda station Jim was still unaware of what had happened in Spain and Colm who had spent the morning, serving teas and coffees listening to the passengers describing a callous killing in Spain, did not realise that they were talking about Gareth. At the end of his shift he picked up a newspaper and was shocked when he realised who had been murdered. He rang Kevin and agreed to meet them in Declan's shop. They spent some time discussing the situation before finally accepting that there was nothing they could do to change what had happened but agreed to remain silent and watchful. The Spanish police knew, that had Mark not returned home, that they, unaware of any historic problems but knowing that he had come looking for Gareth, would certainly have thought of him as a suspect and arrested him. The had wondered about Luke and Margaret but having watched the camera footage were satisfied that neither of them had left the bar during the time frame of the murder. They had seen Gareth being 'picked up' at the bar but no one would have believed that a killing of that type would have been executed by a woman. While the newsagents was where the conversation, concerning the latest threat to the group, was being held there was a different scenario playing out over at the café. Unknown to the army comrades Anthony and Betty Gleeson had been long-time friends of Lena Nowak having met her shortly after her wedding and over the years she had spent a number of holidays with them. They knew that she was a very troubled lady but had never learned the cause of her distress. They realised that her marriage had been short lived but did not feel that it was the cause of her misery. While together, as they watched her cover her facial birthmark with makeup, they wondered would that be what was causing her to feel inadequate and sad. They had not heard from her for some time until recently when she had arrived unexpectantly at the café. She told them that she was afraid and believed she was in danger. She looked distraught and somewhat different but they put it down to the lateness of the night and her being so worried. As she had always been nervous they did not worry too much about her and knew they could help her next morning. She was unusually quiet and asked to go to bed early. Before dawn they heard her speaking to someone and believing she was on her phone did not disturb her. She was not in the bedroom when they looked for her and afterwards, when they heard of her murder, they were too shocked to tell anyone about her visit. Until the DI had questioned them, about a lady with a suitcase, they had not realised that she had been left outside by Jim Mescal thinking that she had arrived, as usual, by taxi. They knew they should have told him about her but at the time they did not know what to do. Listening to the conversations between customers in the café they began to get a sense of fear among some of their clients. They had not seen any connection between Lena's death and the accidental shooting of Bert but everybody was now connecting both incidents with somebody who had been murdered in Spain. The DI had Jim brought to his office. During their conversation, which revealed nothing in connection with the suitcase, the DI asked him what his reaction to Gareth's death was. Up to that point Jim had not heard of the murder and thought it was some time of trick being played on him by the DI. As he refused to comment the DI, not realising this, wondered if somehow he could have had something to do with it. It suddenly dawned on him that, being in the station he may not have known about it, may not have heard what had happened so he handed him the newspaper containing the news. Jim could not believe what he was reading, the graphic description of the scene conjured all types of ideas in his head and for the first time since Lena's murder he wondered had it to do with their past. In the meantime Jack was not having any luck at the B&B as he could not get an answer. He was about to leave when he remembered that Denis lived close by and had also had an opportunity to handle the suitcase when bringing Lena to the house near the carpark. He called to him and was surprised to learn that Lena had a large and a small case. He told Jack, he could only fit the smaller of the two into his car, so he had asked her to leave the larger at the B&B to collect later. She transferred a few items and did as he had asked. He told Jack that the case did not contain very much and had been light to carry. The DI suggested asking the international division, who had located her brother when they needed to have her identified, to get in touch with the family of the deceased so that arrangements could be made to have her buried. As time went by and there had been no response from her family a news bulletin was put out looking for any relatives of Lena Nowak. Within a few hours a man presented himself at the station claiming to be her husband. He told the DI that they had only got married so that she could inherit a large sum of money which they shared. It was never intended that they would stay together and they split up once the cash was received. This contradicted the original story, that her brother told, of her coming on holidays to find her husband. Had she ever come or was the whole story a fabrication? He said that he had not been in touch with her for many years but felt he would like to see her before she was buried. The DI, questioning him learned that she had no family as both her parents were dead, as was her only brother who had died, while serving in the army, shortly before the wedding. The DI told him that could not be true as her brother had identified her shortly after the murder. This caused a lot of confusion leaving the DI wondering if this person was actually her husband or had the body been identified by an imposter. Checking his passport the DI confirmed that he was Antoni Nowak and left him asking himself why would somebody say that he was her brother and wish to falsely identify a corpse. With many thoughts going through his head the DI escorted Antoni to the morgue where a much bigger shock awaited him as he heard him say, "That is not my wife, that is not Lena." "How can you be so sure when you have not seen her in all that time." Taking a wedding photograph from the back of his passport he pointed out a very distinctive birth mark on her face and said, " you could not mistake that even after all this time." Walking out of the morgue Antoni left a bewildered DI pondering on the consequences that would follow this latest information. If it was not his wife then who was she? Could it be another person with the same name? The photograph on the passport certainly looked like her and did not show any birthmark on her face. Could the person who had identified her actually have been her brother? Was there a possibility that he could have been the murderer and no relation what so ever? Which person had stayed in the B&B? who was it that Jim had driven to the café? Was it Antoni's wife Lena or this other woman lying in the morgue? How many more connections to the armed forces would they find? Where was she now? It was time to interview the B&B landlady and the café owners. The DI went to interview the landlady and was dumbfounded as he listened to her say, "that lady called and picked up her things only the other day she apologised for not getting back sooner but had been delayed while visiting a relative." "Are you certain that it was the same lady" he asked her. "Oh yes" she answered, "I could not have mistaken that birthmark on her face." As he made his way back to the station he wondered if the assumptions they had been working on were all incorrect. It looked like the corpse still in the morgue after eight weeks was not the person they thought she was originally. Jim had been absolutely certain that he had left the woman at the cafe so it was time for some tough talking with Anthony and Betty Gleeson. Learning, from the DI, that it had not been her friend Lena that had been murdered came as almost as big a shock to her as when she had heard of the murder. Overcome by emotion she was not able to conceal her feelings and the DI knew that she had not told him the truth at their last interview. Explaining how she had been her friend for many years, she said that she had not known how to react when she had been questioned. She now admitted to having given her a bed the night before the murder but somebody had called with whom she had left, very early, the next morning and she had not heard from her since. This tied in with Jim's account of that night and left the DI wondering who the customer was that told them that Lena had been taken into the back room. Anthony, when questioned, once again denied all knowledge of him. The DI reminded them of the serious consequences that withholding information could have and advised them to give a full account of Lena's time with them. Later reading through their statements the DI saw no reference to a suitcase and wondered if the lady had taken it with her. With DS Tobin he drove over to the café and enquired about it. Betty invited them into the back room and said that she did not honestly know but went into the bedroom to have a look. She reappeared in about two minutes pulling a small case behind her. It had been under the bed and contained just a few cosmetic items which surprised the DI and Betty alike. Jack enlightened them by revealing how a second case had been left at the B&B and could possibly have been big enough to carry whatever Lena had left to be collected. He requested to see the room and was satisfied that it had been the only case that was there. He could not see any other contents so concluded that there had either not been any more or they had been disposed of. They took the case back for a forensic examination. That it was not Lena that had been murdered left him thinking that perhaps the other incidents were not connected or that the whole thing was staged to give the impression that it had been her that had died. If that was the case then it was a very elaborate deception and he wondered who it was that it was designed to convince. At the back of his mind, the family name connecting Both Kevin Burke alias Alfonsi Nowak and Lena Nowak, was constantly reminding him to look at both their backgrounds and see if he could tie them together in some way. He appreciated that Jack was very good at research and, on his return to the station, he delegated that job to him. He decided to have a talk with the super and they both agreed that it was a very strange and perplexing case.

CHAPTER THIRTY-FOUR

Unexpected Relationships

Jack had no idea where to start, should he look for information on the Lena Nowak who was obviously still alive or on Lena Nowak the corpse who remained in the morgue. The DI had asked him to consider the possibility of a liaison with Alfonsi Nowak but did not specify to which of the Lena's he was referring. If there was a partnership with the living Lena could that indicate a combined plan of murder? Could a relationship with the Lena lying in the morgue give reason to believe that the shooting of Bert Delaney was not an accident but a reprisal? What was the possibility of Gareth's murder being associated with it? Thinking, that if he could find a motive for her murder, it might help to pinpoint the killer, he decided to begin by checking the background of the lady in the morgue. Believing that it was her brother who had identified her he made finding him his top priority. With the assistance of the international division he achieved this and with a lot of persuasion convinced the super to allow him to visit him. The local police were very helpful allowing him to use their police station and kindly provided an interpreter. He learned that while recovering from a mental breakdown his sister had met Lena who was also undergoing treatment in the hospital. Both of them, having identical names and suffering with severe depression, latched on to each other and recovered together. He told Jack that at the time he and Lena were homeless having spent all their money on hospital fees trying to overcome her illness. They could not believe it when Lena offered them her house, which was lying empty, to live in until such time as they were in a position to get one of their own. He was on a list for one of the army houses but had to wait until one was available. They had remained in contact and earlier in the year Lena had called and asked his sister to do her a favour. It was a strange request but as she had been so good to them they decided it could be done. She explained to them that she had planned to go to Ireland to locate her husband, without him being aware of it. She told them that he had left her shortly after their wedding but she would like to see him again. She had made arrangements to have some treatment on her face but her appointment had coincided with her visit and so she could not go herself. She was sure that as they had the same name and looked alike she could pass herself off as her and make all the enquires necessary to find him. She paid for the travel and arranged a B&B for her to stay in. She had gone to a lot of trouble explaining what Lena was to do and who she should speak to. She told her not to go into bars or hotels but to eat in the B&B where she had already paid for her food. She told her that she had a friend in the local café and if she felt in any danger to go there. As she spoke good English she knew that she would not have any problem communicating. Before she left Lena told her that she would be contacted once she got to the B&B. That was the last he had seen of her before having to identify her body in the morgue. He had never heard of Alfonsi Nowak and was sure that they did not have any relatives with that name. While he was being interviewed he realised that he had never learned anything about Lena and had no idea where she lived or who her friends were. He told Jack that when he heard that they were going to meet he had brought a letter which his sister had received from Lena some time ago which she had written while, once again, in hospital being treated for her mental disorder. On having this translated to him Jack became aware that Lena, when writing, was in a state of disillusionment. It left him thinking that in her condition could she have been responsible for what had happened. Would there have been something that happened in the past that caused her to have this type of disorder. He told the DS that he did not understand why she had been murdered. He said that he was also worried about the house as he could not get in touch with

Lena and did not know if he could still stay there. The DS advised him to remain there as he was sure that whatever had happened Lena would get in touch with him soon. He advised him to ask Lena to get in touch with him also whenever he saw her. He doubted very much if he would ever get that call. On his journey home he remembered that Anthony and Betty Gleeson had been her friends and wondered could they shed any light on her condition. Having advised the super of his findings he went to the café to have a chat with them. Betty said that she had been aware of her being distracted at times and wondered had it to do with her worrying about her appearance. She spent a lot of time trying to cover her birthmark with makeup. She had never spoken of her background but they felt her marriage breakup was not a big deal for her. They had often wondered why she would not go out for a meal or even a walk on her visits. She often received calls but they did not think that she ever made any. On an odd occasion she had ordered a taxi and spent some hours out of the house. She never spoke of who she had gone to see. One day on her last visit, out of the blue, she went out for a hike in the woods and on returning said she had met a Joe Goode who lived close to the forest. He had invited her in for a cup of tea and they had a great chat. As far as they could remember that was the only time she had spoken about meeting anybody. Leaving them he thought a visit to Joe Goode might reveal something. Joe was rather defensive as he wondered what this was all about. "Living here beside the forest means I get to speak to many people and it would be hard to remember any particular lady." "Joe, this lady had a distinctive birth mark on her face and said that she had a lovely conversation with you." "Is there a reason for these questions, what exactly are you looking for." "Joe, we have reason to believe that this lady may not be well and we are just trying to ascertain how people found her when last they spoke to her." Jack heard Joe say, "She was a very troubled person who, because I was a complete stranger, confided in me. She said that she was on holidays but needed to speak to a doctor in connection with a mental problem that she felt was once again becoming problematic. I gave her the address of the medical centre, where I knew there was a mental disorder clinic, and she went on her way. I have not seen her since. Once again, as the DS left, Joe made a phone call and was relieved to be told that there was no need to worry as everything was under control. The DI felt that everything was beginning to revolve around, what could be, a very disturbed person. Going to the clinic and explaining it was a murder enquiry he was given access to her files. As she had only been looked after there on one occasion they did not have much information about her. The most important thing he observed was the name of the hospital where she had been treated along with the deceased woman. Getting in touch with the police, with whom he had met when interviewing the brother of the lady in the morgue, he made arrangements to visit again and asked to speak with the doctors at the hospital. Their records showed a woman, who for many years, had suffered badly. On one of her stays there she said that she felt responsible for a death but was not sure if she had caused it. Sometimes while sleeping, having been sedated, she would seem to have violent dreams and often call out names of those she was dreaming about. The medical team tried to get her to elaborate when she was awake but she always denied knowing anybody with those names. They were always recorded and Jack was not surprised to see Alfonsi, Jim and Bert among the names. Another reason to believe that the comrades did know each other many years before. Seeing the army comrades listed put him to thinking that something may have happened while they were all together in the army. With the assistance of the police he made enquiries at the local army barracks and having given them the name of Lena Nowak was lucky to find records from around the time of their involvement. An incident involving a soldier by the name of Tobias Gorski going absent without leave had been recorded and there was no sign of him ever returning. It showed his next of kin as Lena Gorski his sister who was also serving in the same unit. She had married a Tobias Nowak around the same time. Remembering Lena's husband saying that her brother had died, while in the army, gave him reason to wonder was this the death that had caused Lena so much trauma? Did he actually die or had he set it all up so as to avoid finishing his term in the army? Would the army comrades have known about it and was this what was the cause of the on-going problems? Once again Jack returned back to the station and reported all that he had Luke and Margaret

While he had been away Luke and Margaret, on holidays in Spain, were trying to come to terms with Gareth's death. They could not help but think that they might have saved his life had they approached him that night instead of putting it off. If the killer had not taken the diamonds would they still be in the room or have been taken by the police? What was the motive for killing him? Had it anything to do with the diamonds? Was the lady they saw walking with him to his room responsible or was she just a distraction? Not knowing of his association with the army they never thought further than robbery. Their weekend of celebration had been ruined and they returned home rather deflated. Arriving back they heard of Jim's arrest on a murder charge and wondered if their world was falling down around them. It was now obvious that Gareth had never intended bringing him the diamonds and with Jim being held in prison it looked like somebody was determined to stop him succeeding in making any money. He cursed Charlotte and blamed her for causing all his hardship. Margaret, bringing him back to the yacht, helped him, in her usual way, to relax. She finally convinced him to put it all behind them and regroup.

CHAPTER THIRTY-FIVE

Complications

In the incident room the super was trying desperately to untangle things. How had a single murder become so complicated? Was it really necessary to consider Bert's shooting and Gareth's murder in the same investigation? Jack had turned up some startling facts but was it still necessary for him to look at Alfonsi Novak's background? Would it make any difference if it turned out that he was related to Lena? She could not understand if Lena Nowak had stayed in the B&B, where would the murder victim have been staying? Why had Lena asked Jim to leave her at the café and not returned to the B&B? It was a most frustrating situation and she hoped things would clear up soon. Jack was back on his computer with thoughts of doing a background check on Alfonsi Nowak when he was notified that another body had been found in the forest. Going to almost the same spot as Lena's body had been found they were confronted with the corpse of a man. Unlike Lena he had been strangled. After the usual on-site examination Dr Taylor agreed to allow the DI to have the body removed. The one person they had failed to interview, Colm O'Hara the buffet attendant, had met his untimely death. A search of the area was almost completed when an officer picked up a key. It had an unusual shape; no markings and it was not known if it had anything to do with the murder. It was bagged and taken back to the station. With another of the army comrades murdered the super had no option but to accept that a link, between them and the killings, may exist. She had no idea what that link could be but thought that at least it might point them in the right direction.

That this murder had a profound effect on the remaining group members would be an understatement as they struggled to understand the significance of it. Who among them would want to see them dead. They could not think of a reason, other than the secret they shared, for this happening and wondered why, after all this time, somebody felt it necessary to seek atonement. Kevin asked Declan and Marge to hold a meeting after they closed the shop. With Gareth dead in Spain and now Colm dead, Jim in prison and Bert in hospital there was only the three of them to meet. Discussing the situation they could only draw a few conclusions. Lena, they believed, was still alive but they thought that she had tried to give the impression that she had been murdered. Mark had not been part of the original group and although they knew that he was aware of their past they eliminated him as a possible suspect or intended victim. The only other person that had known about their past was Jakub Gorski and as far as they knew he was out of the country. "If it has anything to do with our past then that just leaves the three of us. I am sure none of us have had an opportunity of committing these crimes so that only leaves Lena who I do not believe could have done them alone." Marge thought for a moment and then said, "What about her husband, Antoni, as far as we know he did not share our secret but have you given any thought to him? He could have been operating with her or for her." They had to agree that they had not thought of him and he had never come into the equation. They still could not understand why! What had changed to bring on this madness? What could they do to avoid becoming victims themselves? Kevin said, "We will have to locate both Antoni and Lena and hope we can put a stop to it all." Declan spoke out and said, "That is a tall order seeing that none of us have been in contact with either of them for so long. How do you visualise going about it?" "At this moment I do not have an idea but we will have to come up with something." They had to accept that although it looked as if it was connected to their past it may not be. They finished talking and left everything in abeyance until morning. Leaving them Kevin was satisfied that neither of them thought of him as being the killer and he was sure that neither of them would have done it.

Meanwhile Mark as he sat at home contemplating his future was not bothered by the fact that he had not been invited to the meeting with Declan and Marge at the shop. He had nothing to do with their past and would not now be involved with them in the future. He wondered about Gareth but was not convinced that his death had anything to do with what was happening around him. In securing his Amsterdam objective Gareth had, unwittingly, involved some serious criminals, who known how much cash he had received, would have had no hesitation in taking it from him even if it involved murder. It was a question now of whether he would go it alone, which was always difficult, or team up with somebody leaving the possibility of him being used again. As he had many contacts and some good friends he decided to take a chance and start off on his own. Firstly he must move to a new area where he would not be recognised and from there begin the next phase in his life.

In the meantime Jim still pleading his innocence was being held in custody awaiting further questioning. He thought that he should say who had given him the handbag to dump but kept putting it off believing that the murderer would be found and he would be released. He could not quite come to terms with Gareth's death and was torn between thinking it had more to do with his diamond smuggling than his past. His solicitor was applying for bail but he did not think it would be possible for him to raise the type of money required. On hearing of Colm's murder he thought he would be safer staying in custody until everything settled down. Not having heard that it was not the Lena Nowak whom he had known that had been murdered he really did not understand what was going on. Was it just a coincidence that two of his friends had been killed around the same time? Could he believe that a murder in Spain and the two beside him were connected? Should he consider himself in danger and if so by whom? What a mess he thought and decided that once he was released he would move far away, get a job and forget about crime.

CHAPTER THIRTY-SIX

Jack Looking For Answers

Thoughts, by Jack, now focused on Kevin Burke, formally known as Alfonsi Nowak, as he scanned his computer for knowledge. Not ever having been in trouble and not having been vetted for the security job there was no information on Alfonsi Nowak available on the Garda system. If he was to obtain anything worthwhile he believed that he would have to go back and have a talk with Kevin's army CO. Commandant Harris, who on receiving his call, invited him to the barracks and told him he would hopefully be in a position to help him. Being an astute person with an enquiring mind he had followed the case as it unfolded and on seeing the reports of Jacks visits abroad, got in touch with Alfonsi's previous CO and collected a lot of information. He had been told that Alfonsi Nowak was an exemplary soldier and had risen to the rank of sergeant very quickly. He was a top marksman and following his two years national service, most of it served with the United Nations, decided to live in Ireland. He joined the Irish army and became an Irish citizen. The DS knew his history after that so thanking the CO he headed back to the station. The noticeboard in the incident room had taken on a new look with most of the original names replaced by the latest suspects. What had started with a single murder had turned more difficult as the second one occurred. It was now a double killing but as yet nothing to link them together. Both had happened at almost the same location but other than that, there was no evidence to suggest any connection between them. Although Gareth had been part of the army comrades and involved with the international investigation there did not seem to be any evidence to tie his murder with those of Lena or Colm. The DI was wondering what exactly had DS Tobin found out about Lena and Alfonsi and would the information help to solve the case. The most important thing was he had established the fact that all the names associated with the army comrades had been together at the time of Tobias Gorski's disappearance. Whether or not this would help with the investigation only time would tell.

Other factors complicating the issues surrounding the murders were adding to the frustration being felt by the super and DI. The high-level Garda investigation at the casino seemed to have fizzled out with Gareth now deceased. Jim in custody and Colm now also deceased seemed to have had some level of involvement with both investigations. Having two women with the same name, one alive and one in the morgue was indeed both strange and unusual. Then there were the army comrades with a least two of the deaths associated with them. Would they ever get the break they needed to tie it all together and see justice being served. While their investigation carried on, the police in Spain were working to identify Gareth's killer. They could not find a single clue in his room and concentrated on looking for a suspect on the CCTV films. Many people had passed in and out of the hotel but any interviewed were quickly eliminated from the investigation. Knowing he had been involved in an illegal diamond smuggling transaction they were convinced that it was a gang style killing and felt that they would be very lucky to find the killer. They kept the file open but wasted no more time looking for a suspect.

With the Casino investigation over Charlotte was back working in her station and once again free to meet Jack. Their evenings were spent happily going to shows, dancing or having a few drinks in the local. One evening, as they sat watching the news on the tele, they saw a report of a gang land assassination and they started to discuss the case Jack was involved in. Going through all the names she was amazed to see how many of them were involved in both the smuggling and the murder cases but nothing significant was spoken about until she heard of the unusual key found at the site of Colm's murder. Asking Jack to describe it to her she said that it sounded like those in use at the casino. Following her advice, the next day, Jack advised the DI and retrieving the key they made their way to the casino. Speaking to the manager they learned that Kevin Burke, saying that the recent murders had made him nervous, had asked to have the lock on his door changed. The old lock was in the store but he did not know if the key was with it. No key was found with the lock but the one found in the forest was a perfect match. Would this, on its own, be sufficient to tie Kevin with the murder? That it was found close to the murder site was staggering but it could have been dropped before the murder had taken place or even placed there to implicate him. The DI, advising the manager not to reveal what he had just witnessed, decided to talk to the super and see how she felt about it. Knowing, that Kevin had been involved in the kidnapping and could certainly have been in the woods when Lena had been murdered, she wondered were both murders connected and if he had some involvement in them. Having interviewed him on a number of occasions they both knew how difficult he was and thought it would be better to accumulate some more evidence before calling him in again. Jack was given the task of looking through phone call records made or received by Kevin. While he was doing this the super and the DI held another interview with Jim and came to the conclusion that he had no part in Lena's murder. They had never learned who had given him the bag he had dumped in the skip but thought it would all come to light as their enquiries continued. They advised his solicitor that they were releasing him on bail, making it quite clear that he was still under suspicion and waiting for a court case involving his part in the kidnapping so he could not travel anywhere without notifying them.

 Jim, not sure what type of reception he would receive from Kevin, almost asked to be kept in. His thoughts jumped from Kevin to Luke as he remembered what had happened to Gareth and he wondered had Luke anything to do with his death. He needed to speak to Denis and find out everything that had gone on while he had been detained. He was afraid to go to the casino in case he might be seen by either Luke or Kevin so opted to call to Denis's house. He was taken aback when he heard that Luke, Margaret and Mark had all been in Spain at the time of Gareth's murder but the authorities there had cleared them all of any misdoing. He had not seen any of them at the casino but Luke's yacht was still moored at the harbour so he assumed that he was not too far away. Kevin, he said, had intended leaving his job and going back home but as he was implicated in the kidnapping his passport had been confiscated and he could not go anywhere. Jim then heard him say "I think you should have a conversation with him as he seems quite worried about your safety." Jim knew that Kevin would have been more concerned about the possibility of him telling where he had picked up the bag and would be relieved to hear that he had not said a word. He went over to the casino but Kevin had a day off and had gone to see Bert in hospital so Jim did not get to see him. He wondered how Declan and Madge were coping with all that had happened and thought it would be a good idea to go over and see them. They were still in shock and wanted to know if he felt that the murders were all linked to their past. They heard him say "If the lady murdered in the forest had been Lena I would answer yes to that question. That Colm, who had no connections with that lady, was strangled at almost the same spot, to me, indicates that there is a random murderer out there who the Gardai should be looking for. Gareth was killed, far away in Spain, by a criminal gang who knew he had all those diamonds and nothing to do with the murders here. I will not be going into the woods until someone is caught but I do not believe it has anything to do with us or our pledge of silence." Seeing that they were still not sure he reminded them that when Colm was murdered Bert was in hospital, he was in jail, Gareth was in Spain and he assumed that Lena was nowhere near so that only left Kevin and the two of them who could have committed the crime. He said to them " where either of you involved or do you believe that Kevin committed these murders." They denied having been in the forest, although they knew that Declan had gone out walking that evening and said that they could not believe that Kevin could do anything like that. They relaxed a little before he left and they hoped that what he had said made sense. Madge remained apprehensive as she also knew that Declan had gone out on the evening before Colm's body had been discovered. Deep inside she believed that he had nothing to do with it, but with so many strange happenings going on around her, a little doubt lingered and it was impossible to fully relax. Jim had not realised that his every move had been watched since leaving the station and a report of where he went sent to the DI. The DI found it very interesting that one of his visits had been to the newsagents as, up to now, he had not tied Declan with the army comrades, the kidnaping or the murder. Jack pointed out that he may have only gone there for the paper but the DI said that he intended to follow it up. Jack, who had spent the morning looking through phone records, reminded the DI that Madge had said something about his army background and they wondered had he also been involved with them all those years before. Why, now that they knew the murdered woman was not who they had believed her to be, would they still be so nervous? If they had thought that their friend had been murdered because of something that had happened a long time ago would they not now realise that it was a random attack with nothing tying it to their past? If there had been an incident, in the past, how bad could it have been if after all this time, it still caused them so much grief? If Antoni had not left so suddenly, without leaving any way of contacting him, perhaps he could have enlightened them. On the other hand perhaps he was aware of the incident causing all this trauma and did not wish it to be known that he was also hiding a secret. Did this woman loose her life because she was mistaken for someone else? Could she have been mistaken for a woman, who was also known as Lena Nowak and was, in some way, tied up with the army comrades? Thinking that this may be one scenario the DI believed that he would have to find her husband and get a lot more background information on her. Remembering that the last time he had turned up was following a news bulletin the DI tried to contact him with the same method.

CHAPTER THIRTY-SEVEN

Having Doubts About Joe Goode

The following morning Jack, while on his way towards the station, stopped to buy a newspaper and could not believe how nervous Madge was when she saw him. That he was only in the shop to get a paper seemed to relieve her and he wondered why she should have reacted in that way. Had Declan learned something which they did not want him to find out about? Had she been threatened but could not say? Perhaps, he thought, the two murders so close had un-nerved her and she was feeling vulnerable. He decided that while he was looking up phone records he would look up hers also and see if he could link them to a source that might help him to discover the reason for her dismay. Most of her calls were connected to their suppliers but the one that concerned him was a number of calls to Joe Goode and he wondered why they would keep in touch. Cross referencing those with Joe's own records he found two calls made, by Joe, to an unfamiliar number and both lasting less than thirty seconds. At first he thought that he may have dialled an incorrect number and had just hung up but felt that it would be unlikely for that to happen twice, on different occasions, to the same number. As he was due to meet the DI he made a note of the numbers, call times and duration with the intention of checking them out after his meeting. The super, DI and Jack, not having anything definite to go on, spent the morning reviewing all the evidence they had. In an attempt to make some sense of what had happened they checked their interview evidence, dates of visits to all those that may have been involved, connections between the casino investigation, Lucy's kidnapping and Bert's shooting. No matter how hard they tried they could not find the link they so desperately needed. At some point they referenced their visits to Joe Goode but as he was never considered in the frame they passed over it without paying much attention. That Colm had been murdered and Bert shot it did put the army comrades to the front of the investigation but as yet there was nothing definite to tie them to either murder. Gareth's death, in Spain, although he was part of the comrades was not considered to be connected. The DI had a deep feeling that Lena Nowak, Antoni's wife, was at the root of their search for an answer and thought that if her husband failed to turn up it would be necessary to visit her homeland again and delve deeper into her background.

Jack, whose whole life since joining the force, centred around his work could not believe how distracted he became when thoughts of Charlotte flashed across his mind. He wondered how the most beautiful girl he had ever seen could possibly have been interested in him. His life had changed drastically since meeting her and now instead of worrying about his job he spent a lot of his time dreaming of their future. Although only a short time together they were planning on buying a house, getting married and starting a family. What a beautiful stage it was in their lives.

With the phone records in front of him he once again began to give them his attention and remembered his note on Joe Goode. The dates of his calls coincided with the visits that the DI and himself had made to him and set Jack wondering would they be linked. The numbers were not listed, which immediately started alarm bells ringing, and on contacting the phone providers he was advised that the number had been withdrawn as it was not in use any more. The name of the customer had been Bona Kowasti a name totally unknown to Jack. He wondered if his first thoughts that Joe had rung the wrong number was correct. He continued checking the different records but found nothing to give him cause to believe that they were in any way related to their murders. Back at the station he asked the DI what he thought of the calls made by Joe and on looking at the dates and times the inspector felt that it was too much of a coincidence that they both were made on the days of their visits. He was very interested in the name of the person that Joe had rung and having studied it for a few minutes told Jack that it was an anagram of Antoni Nowak. This was something new they had learned and off to Joe Goode's cottage they headed. He was dumbfounded and could not understand how they had found out that he had rung Antoni. Joe, under pressure of being taken to the station for questioning, explained that since hearing of him meeting Lena, Antoni had asked him, if Lena was visiting, to watch out for her as although they were no longer together, he worried about her constantly. Her mental health was a great concern to him and he tried to watch her, from a distance, as best he could. When asked why he felt it necessary to make the calls on the days that they had called he replied that he thought it might help Antoni to locate and help her. This worried the DI as he knew that the identity of the corpse was not known when first they had visited him. Why would her husband take an interest in her after all those years? Why would Joe ring him about their visit without knowing who the murdered woman was? Did he know more than he was saying? Explaining that they wished to speak to Antoni they asked Joe for his address. "I'm sorry but I have never known where he lived, all I ever had was his phone number." I can give you that if it would help. Realising that Joe was not aware of the number being invalid they accepted his offer and wondered would he try to ring it when they left.

As they left his house Jack related the experience he had on going to the shop that morning and the DI thought it a good idea for them both to return and see if there was any reaction. Declan and not Marge was looking after the customers when they arrived and showed no sign of nervousness. He greeted them in his usual manner just adding that Madge was lying down as she had not been feeling too good. Out of the blue he told them that she was suffering with the same symptoms as she had many years ago while a medic in the army. This stunned them both as they had never considered her being part of the army group. Jack now wondered did her phone calls to Joe Goode have a greater significance than he had imagined and would she also share a secret if there was one? Telling Declan to wish her well they headed back to the station feeling that they had something else to consider in connection with this case.

CHAPTER THIRTY-EIGHT
Kevin Visits Bert

Kevin went to the hospital to visit Bert not knowing what he was hoping for but knew that whatever way he found him it would not change the situation. How could he judge Bert's condition? Would the medical staff be willing to give him any information? Not having heard from his two MP friends he wondered had they been taken off ward duty and were unable to observe him. If Bert had regained his memory should he tell him all that had happened? Arriving at the hospital he, like the DI on his visit, was escorted to a private room where Bert was still sitting in a wheelchair unable to do anything for himself. He failed to recognise Kevin but he learned, from one of the MPs looking after him, that the doctors had seen an improvement and were hopeful that in time he would regain at least part of his memory. He heard him say, "at the moment he is being kept partially sedated to give his brain a chance to recover and that is why he is unable to recognise or communicate with you." Kevin could not decide whether this was good or bad news but it did mean that he would have to continue visiting him regularly and watch him. He left the room feeling a little distressed, not knowing that Bert who had recovered part of his memory, had told the staff that he did not wish to speak to him. As he drove back towards the casino he thought about Jim and worried about what, if anything, he had revealed to the Gardai. He was relieved on arriving back to get a note from him telling of his visit and a promise to call again that afternoon. He knew that if Jim had divulged anything, during his interviews, he would not be calling to see him. That neither he nor Jim could travel anywhere gave them an opportunity to take a serious look at what had happened and hopefully come up with some way of dealing with it. Later that day, during their conversation, Jim continued to say that he believed they were over reacting because of their secrecy vow and thought the murders were in no way related. Kevin agreed with him and thought they should relax and go back to doing things as they had done previously. Kevin, having said goodbye to Jim, rang Declan and told him about his visit to the hospital. Both Declan and Madge wondered, if Bert was improving, why he had not recognised Kevin who had gone to visit him just after the accident. Was he telling them the truth or had he some reason for hiding Bert's condition? Madge thought that Declan should make an appointment to visit him and see for himself. They had not been aware that on that previous occasion, as he was so ill, Kevin had not been allowed to see him. Kevin, knowing of the friendship between Betty and Lena, went to the café for a chat with them. With Betty, under doctors' orders, confined to bed and Anthony busy he had to wait a while for his chat. Drinking his coffee and listening to the customers talking about the local murders he felt very strange especially as he knew that they would have had no way of knowing that he knew the victims. He heard so many theories, so many ideas, would any of them come close to the truth? He finally got a chance to speak to Anthony who told him that the murdered woman, who they had thought was Lena, had arrived late on the Friday evening and had gone off early the following morning. He said that they thought they had heard her speaking to someone on her phone but had not been aware that she had gone until they had looked for her later. "Have you seen or heard from Antoni" Kevin asked, which Anthony thought a strange question as he had not kept in touch with him since he had broken up with Lena. "No" he answered "Is there some reason why I should have. Has he been here recently?" Kevin said, "I believe he was the one that told the DI that the body in the morgue was not Lena so I have to believe that he has been here." Replying Anthony said, "I did wonder how the Gardai got to know that the body was not who they thought it had been. Do you think that he had anything to do with the murders," Kevin said, "It does seem strange that he suddenly appeared from nowhere and was able to go to the morgue without any of us even knowing he had been here." Replying Anthony said, "Well obviously, if it had been our Lena who had been murdered, I may have agreed that he could have had some involvement but as she is an unknown woman I do not think so." Kevin then asked him, "Could he have mistaken her for his wife." Anthony, getting a little impatient with Kevin said, "Why would he have been here in the first place unless he knew that Lena was here. He would hardly have just been walking around the woods and accidently found someone, that looked like his wife, after all this time. No, that does not make any sense at all." Kevin, sensing some resentment in Anthony's voice, finished his coffee and saying that he would see him soon went out of the café. After closing the café Anthony went up to Betty and told her of Kevin's visit. Although not feeling very well she, being more perceptive than Anthony, wondered how Kevin had thought that they had remained in touch with Antoni. She asked Anthony did he think that Kevin was considering them as possible suspects. They had not been in the army at the same time as the comrades so neither of them knew of the pledge of silence and found it hard to understand why there was so much tension among what was usually a jolly group. Had they heard or seen something that herself and Anthony had missed? Could the rumours circulating regarding a link between the murders have any substance? Anthony suggested having an evening together in the café, as they had on many occasions before, and seeing what their reaction was. Betty said that she would be strong enough by Wednesday and as they closed early each Wednesday that would suit fine. They usually just phoned everyone and so they followed with tradition and got in touch with each of them as usual. It was strange not having Bert, Gareth or Colm with them but all the others arrived with the usual supply of beer and Betty provided the food. Kevin and Jim arrived first and Declan and Madge, having closed the shop, were not long behind them. They had always included Joe Goode in their invitations and he arrived soon afterwards. Declan, not realising that there was anybody else coming, closed the door and pulled the blinds. Betty, thinking this would be a good opportunity to see if there was anything going on between Anthony and Amelia, had invited Patrick and Amelia to join them.

Hearing a knock on the door Anthony went over with the intentions of advising whoever it was that the café was closed. Seeing Patrick and Amelia at the door left him speechless as he heard Betty telling him to let them in that they were joining them for a few drinks. The introduction of these two newcomers into the party had a twofold effect. It certainly showed a close relationship between Anthony and Amelia even though both of them tried hard to disguise it and there was a very definite change in the atmosphere as the rest of the group started to relax. Having, who the group would consider, outsiders ensured that the conversation did not revolve around the murders and helped to make everybody feel more at ease. Anthony, trying to be the perfect host, was left trying to figure out the reason for Betty including Patrick and Amelia. Had it been to distract everyone from a conversation she did not wish to hear or had she set it up to see his reaction to seeing Amelia. As she was with Patrick and he was with Betty they could not show any sign of affection but somehow as they spoke to each other they still seemed to emit a feeling of togetherness not gone unnoticed by Betty. All types of thoughts went through her head as she wondered what she could do to stop Anthony seeing her. Would she follow him one morning and once he realised that she knew he might just abandon his early mornings and late nights? Would she just come out straight and tell him she knew of his romantic interludes and hope that it would put an end to them? She thought of giving him a choice, staying with her or going off with Amelia but was afraid that he may choose to leave her and that is not what she wanted. She wondered what reaction she would get if she spoke to Amelia but had not the courage to do it. She would need more time to think this through before doing anything rash. Joe said that it was getting near his bedtime so Patrick offered to drop him off on his way home. Leaving the original group together it was inevitable that the conversation would focus on Bert's accident and the recent murders. Kevin was upbeat and optimistic as he told them that he had visited Bert and had been told that there was a good chance of him recovering most of his memory. He said that he was extremely saddened by Colm's death and found it hard to come to terms with the fact that it had happened in the same area as the first murder. That there seemed to be no connection between them baffled him and with thoughts that there could be a random murderer around he would not be walking in the forest anytime soon. Jim had also been very saddened by Colm's death and also with his other friend Gareth who had died in Spain. He had heard people link them together but he, knowing both of them, saw no connection whatsoever. Declan agreed with Jim's opinion as he could not put them together either. Betty, thinking of what she would say later to Anthony about his relationship with Amelia, remained out of the conversation while being a perfect hostess handing plates of food and glasses of wine around. Declan and Madge, giving the excuse that they had to get up early to open the shop, bade farewell and headed home. Kevin and Jim first to arrive and now last to leave spent some time on their way home discussing the evening and the topics that had been discussed. They both agreed that it had been organised to prevent friction between everybody. They accepted that they would have to get the remnants of the group together and work out a strategy to ensure no further fatalities. Meanwhile back in the café Anthony was wondering how long it would take before Betty started to chastise him about Amelia. He had seen her watching them and was convinced that she could read his every thought. Would he just admit to his misdemeanour and take whatever punishment he was given? Could he deny everything and hope to get away with it? Would this be the end of his romantic interludes? What had brought her attention to him seeing Amelia? Had she seen them together and kept it to herself? Seeing her coming into the room he prepared himself for the worst and could not believe it when she never said a word. Sitting down to watch the tele as normal she simply said to him "are you not going to watch your favourite programme." He was so shocked that he just sat down without saying a word.

The following morning he decided not to meet Amelia in the forest but as he walked most days he headed out as usual but this time away from the forest. Betty, overnight, had decided to follow him and when he met Amelia to clear the air and see what he would do. She realised that it would be impossible to go on as they were. She could not believe that he was not going in his usual direction and thought they must have realised that she had been watching them and arranged to meet elsewhere. As time went by and there was no sign of him seeing anyone she made her way back to the shop hoping that she had timed it right before he turned around and saw her. Amelia picking her herbs could not believe that he had not turned up and believed that Betty must have stopped him. She knew that Betty had been watching them but thought they had done enough to disguise their feelings. What she had not noticed was Patrick taking an interest in her and Anthony and realising that this was who she was meeting each morning. He followed her as he walked with Snap and was disappointed not to see her meeting anybody. Amelia had seen him following her and felt she had to make a decision on what she really wanted; was it her secure life with Patrick, dreary as it may be, or a new start with Anthony? The thoughts of all the problems that leaving Patrick and with Anthony leaving Betty would create put her in a different frame of mind and at that moment she decided to opt for the secure life. Ringing Anthony she simply said "Good bye Anthony it's time to end our romantic interludes." Anthony was stunned and all he could think of was that Betty had spoken to Amelia but as he put the phone down he felt a great sense of relief. What had started off as a bit of fun, without him realising it, had probably got a little out of hand and he could so easily have ruined his marriage. Betty never quite knew how the transformation had come about but went out of her way to see that it would not happen again. Patrick never did see Amelia in the forest other than when she was picking her herbs and was convinced that he had been mistaken. It looked to Betty that her tactics had worked better than she had planned and she was delighted to see things returning back to normal.

CHAPTER THIRTY-NINE

Who Is Lena?

As the Lena Nowak, who was unknown to the army comrades, lay in the morgue a call was sent out to entice Antoni Nowak to call to the station. The DI was thinking how foolish he had been not getting his address and hoped that he would contact them. If he could accumulate some evidence tying his wife to the army group he might begin to make some headway in the investigation. He was convinced that there had to be a connection that bound them together and if necessary he would travel and find it. DS Tobin had discovered that, at the time that her brother Tobias went missing, they had all been together but they had never found any evidence to show any connection between them since. Everything had changed in the case from when they had interviewed those they thought were involved to when they became aware of what could be a settling of old scores. Looking at the facts was a startling account of two murders close bye, a murder in Spain and an accidental shooting with all, except the murdered woman, being involved with each other in one way or another. That the murdered woman had the same name and looked like the Lena associated with the army comrades lent itself to speculation. Had she been deliberately murdered to give the impression that her double had been killed? Was it that she was mistaken for her double and murdered in error? Why had she been murdered? Where any of the army group involved? Was it a robbery gone wrong? Was it connected to Colm's murder or even to Gareth's death in Spain. Could all the earlier suspects be taken out of the equation? Had Bert's shooting been an attempt on his life and not an accident as reported? If none of these had a motive for the murders could there still be someone unknown out there waiting to strike again? Would the casino key, which they believed had belonged to Kevin Burke, play any part in finding the killer? A phone call from Antoni confirmed that he had left the country and due to work commitments, would not be coming back for some time. He said that he did not think that his wife had been in Ireland and he could not believe that she had anything to do with the murders. He had not been able to contact her but when he did he would get her to get in touch. He told the DI that he did not know any of her previous friends except Bert who had been their best man and who he had kept in contact with over the years. His visit to Ireland, he said, was to see Bert after he had heard of his accident but now realised that it may never be possible to speak to him again. He hung up leaving the DI more determined than ever to get to the bottom of this frustrating case.

CHAPTER FORTY

Statement Retracted

That he had a key which he could link to Kevin started him thinking of what else he would need to get him nearer to arresting him. He thought back and remembered that Jim had never said from who he had received the handbag dumped in the skip. If Kevin had been involved with that bag it would certainly be enough, with the key, to bring him in for questioning. He had Jim picked up and taken to the interview room. Advising him that they had found new evidence in their murder enquiry they asked him once again for the name of the person who had given him the bag that he had dumped in the skip. This time he said that he could not remember so the DI cautioned him and told him he was once again arresting him for the murder of Lena Nowak. You can make one call to your solicitor but this time we will be objecting to bail and you will remain in custody until your trial. You will be happy to know that, having this new evidence, your friend Kevin will join you tomorrow on a similar charge. He got really upset and said, "he is not going to be the cause of me spending years in jail, why should I get the blame for something that I had nothing to do with." The Di, while he had him in that frame of mind, reminded that his fingerprints were on the victim's bank card. "What will happen to me if I tell you who I got the bag from." If you write out a statement and sign it I will release you as soon as we speak to your solicitor." Jim thought about what he should do and being assured that he would be free and the person who gave him the bag would be arrested agreed to make a statement. Seeing the name he had hoped for being written as the person responsible for handing over the bag the DI was overjoyed. Jim insisted on speaking to his solicitor before signing it and as he could not come to the station until the following morning Jim spent the night in a cell. His solicitor, while having a private meeting with Jim before the interview with the Di, reading his statement put it to him that he had been forced into making it and he would advise him not to sign but to tear it up. Jim did not know what to do, if he did not sign it now would he be kept in on a murder charge or worse still would he be released to face a terrible reprisal. Seeing his reluctance to listen to him the solicitor took the statement and told Jim that he would give him until twelve o'clock to decide what direction he intended taking. "If you still feel you want to go down this road and not take my advice the future will be completely in your own hands. Can you imagine, if there is not sufficient evidence to arrest him, what he will think when he hears that you signed a statement naming him as the culprit. It could easily turn out that someone else had given it to him and he had absolutely nothing to do with the murder. How would you feel then?" Jim, at the interview, surprised the DI by saying that he had been mistaken about who he had received the bag from and was now so confused that he could not remember who had given it to him. His solicitor was quick to tell the DI that he was convinced that Jim had been put under undue pressure and he would be taking it up with the Garda ombudsman. He reminded the DI that he had released Jim only a short while ago knowing that there was hardly any chance that he could have committed the crime. Unless you release him again now I will have no option but to take it to a much higher level. The DI, in conjunction with the super, knowing that they could bring him in again if they felt it necessary, decided it would be prudent and cause a lot less stress, for everyone, to release him. He walked out with his solicitor who, when they were out of sight, advised him not to answer any questions or sign any papers unless he was with him. He tore up the unsigned statement and put in in a bin along the street. Jim felt very relieved but realised how close he had come to doing something that could have cost him dearly.

In the station the DI was fuming as he thought how close he had come to getting the evidence against the one person that he so desperately needed. He was not yet totally convinced that he was the murderer but he was certainly one of the top suspects. Always in the back of his mind was the knowledge that, her husband, Antoni had been around and he knew that he could not discount him completely. With Gareth, who he had not considered as he was part of a completely different investigation, having been murdered he had to think that perhaps there was a connection with somebody else in that charity group who may also have been involved. Charlotte had told him that she had seen Luke and Anthony, the café owner, having a long conversation but did not think that they were involved in anything together but he knew how clever these criminals could be and would not discount that possibility either. That Declan and Kevin were friends could mean that Luke may also have known Kevin and the fact that nobody was aware of it did not indicate that they did not operate together at some level. Would that be who he had been seeing when he went out after six on the weekend of Lena's murder. He wondered would Madge have any idea. Once again, along with his DS, he made his way to the newsagents with the intention of asking her if she had any idea who he had been going out to see that evening. Not knowing why he would be asking a question like that she hesitated before saying anything. As she did he asked her if she thought it could have been Kevin Burke or Jim Mescal. Thinking that he was trying to link Declan and these two together she was happy to tell him that it was Mark who he had dealings with. She also told him that they had not seen Mark since Gareth's murder. The DI assured her that his investigation had nothing to do with either herself or Declan and he was very thankful for her co-operation which he hoped would help him overcome some of the difficulties he was experiencing. Knowing that Mark had been involved with Gareth but was not one of the army comrades he began to wonder if perhaps Madge was deliberately trying to prevent him learning of their past or indeed something more recent. He did not realise that neither Declan nor Madge had not been in the army at the same time as the others and knew nothing of their past. Why was he finding it so hard to get answers? Was everyone, involved with the comrades, determined to prevent this murder being solved? Was it just that they did not know who was responsible but were afraid of their original crime, if there had been one, being discovered through this investigation? There was every sign of a closing of ranks which worried him greatly. He wondered if the remaining comrades thought of Gareth's murder in Spain as part of the overall picture and were they worried that they could end up the same way? What was it that bound them together. That Lena, their army comrade, had not been the victim should have relaxed them, even if there had been something relating to her causing them to worry. Like him perhaps they were thinking that the intended victim was Lena and the other woman who ended up being murdered had been mistaken for her.

On their way back to the station Jack, thinking that there could be a link between Kevin and Luke, wondered, if Kevin had been involved in the murders and thought that he was in danger of being arrested, would he try to escape by arranging for Luke to take him away on the yacht. The DI, who was always amazed when Jack came up with these type of thoughts, believed that the idea was well worth considering and if things headed in that direction he would think about having a watch put on the harbour. Jack was delighted to think that the DI had appreciated one of his ideas. He was going off for a few days with Charlotte and would be glad to have a break from this very strange and complicated murder case.

CHAPTER FORTY-ONE

Jack and Charlotte On Holidays

He and Charlotte arrived in Lanzarote at mid-day and although it was early spring the sun was shining and the temperature was a very pleasant twenty-five degrees. The taxi took them from the airport to their hotel in Puerto del Carmen which took about thirty minutes and after checking in they changed into summer clothes and went out for lunch. Swimming and sunbathing was what they both had looked forward to and if the weather remained as it was they would be able to enjoy plenty of that. Walking around the old harbour, hand in hand, they were happy and delighted that everything was working out so well between them. Later that evening, leaving the bar, they made their way to their room knowing that the night would bring them magic as they held each other close. They had never been on holiday together before and although they had often spent the night together this felt totally different. It was as if they were just meeting for the first time and the excitement they both felt was electric. Hugging and kissing each other they gradually removed the few summer clothes they were wearing and stood together under the warm scented shower. Thoughts of any work-related problems were forgotten as they delighted in running their hands over each other's body washing their cares away. The hotel bed, to their delight, was dressed with cool silk sheets and having dried each other they lay together just enjoying the feeling of togetherness. Being so close, and very much in love, nature took over and before falling asleep in each other's arms, they enjoyed a most beautiful period of lovemaking. The following day as they walked along the promenade people seeing them could not help but see how much in love they were. They radiated happiness and were a joy to meet. Their holiday week ended but their love had risen to a new high and they could not wait to complete plans for their future together. Arriving home was an anti-climax and after just two lonely days Jack moved from home and into Charlotte's apartment.

Declan, on Madge's insistence, rang to make an appointment to visit Bert. He was advised that Bert was having extensive therapy and would not be allowed visitors for a couple of days. He explained that he was a friend and an ex-army comrade and he would like to see him as soon as possible. "Ring back next week and you will be advised further" is what he heard before the phone was put down and he was cut off. As he was about to go back into the shop the phone rang and Joe Goode asked him if he could come over to his house as he needed to talk to him. Explaining, to Madge, why he could not go to the hospital he told her that Joe had asked him to call to his house. Arriving there he was at once aware that Joe was upset and worried about something. "Declan the DI called and somehow he knew that I had been ringing Antoni, when he left I tried to ring Antoni again but the number is not available. Has he been in touch with you or Madge." Answering him Declan said, "Joe we have not heard from him for a long time and only heard the other evening that he had been here. Why are you so worried? He has probably just gone back home." "It's just that he had asked me to let him know if there was anyone looking for him or making enquiries about Lena. There is one other thing that is worrying me, the DI had the dates that I had called Antoni and asked me why I had made the calls on the same day as he and the DS had called here to see me. I told him that I was hoping to help him look after Lena but that day was before they had a name for the dead woman. If he asks me how I knew who she was what can I tell him." "The best way out of this is to tell the truth, tell him you have always kept in touch and that a woman had been murdered did not make any difference. You can say that you did not connect the murdered woman with Lena until you heard her name which was a long time after you had made the phone call." "Do you think he would believe that" Joe asked Declan. "He has no reason not to and I'm sure he does not think that you had anything to do with the murder. Do not worry about the phone not being active if Antoni needs to get in touch, as before, he knows your number." Leaving a more relaxed Joe Goode at the cottage he went back to the shop where he related all to Marge. She was curious to know if Joe could have known the murdered woman's name and if he did who had told him. She realised that if he had been speaking to Antoni then without them being aware of it he had been close by and that left her wondering had he anything to do with the murder. Knowing that Antoni had, for many years, been concerned with Lena's health and tried to help her she put those thoughts out of her head especially when she considered that he would not have mistaken his own wife.

CHAPTER FORTY-TWO
Which Lena?

The incident room was a hive of activity with the super, DI and DS all, once again, trying to pull things together. The super was thinking that Antoni could have been a key component of this case and was disturbed that he had been let go so easily. She felt that the least they should have done was interview him. The DI pointed out that he had told them that the corpse was not his wife so why should they have thought that he was involved in a stranger's death. It was obvious that he and Lena had not been together for many years so perhaps questions regarding his coming to see her body could have been asked. Remembering Joe Goode saying that Antoni still worried about her and was in Ireland might lend itself to thinking that Lena was also visiting. Jack suggested that they should be concentrating on the murdered woman and looking for a reason for her being here. "You are of course right Jack and indeed we must find out definitively who stayed at the B&B and who was brought to the café. That Lena had a prominent birthmark on her face should have made it easy to distinguish between them." The DI thought for a moment and then said, "I think it is time to speak to the B&B owner and see if she can shed any light on it. She said that the woman had stayed with her before the murder and that the same lady had come back to collect her belongings about two weeks following the killing. It could not have been the same person unless Lena herself had stayed there and not the murdered woman." Jack asked if they remembered Dr Taylor passing a remark about an unusual purple colour on the dead woman's face and he wondered could that have been an attempt to duplicate the birthmark and fool everyone. The super and DI looked at each other and agreed that Jack had an uncanny way of spotting and remembering the obscure things. Asking Dr Taylor to meet them at the morgue they drove over to have a talk with him. Dr Taylor told them that during the post-mortem he had scraped some of the substance from her face and placed it in a phial which when analysed it proved to be a form of makeup and he had not paid further attention to it. Taking out photographs of the corpse as she looked on arrival at the morgue showed a distinctive purple shading on the right side of her face. They all agreed that a day out in the open would have caused a deterioration and were convinced that it could certainly have looked like a birthmark earlier. If that was the case they had to believe that she was sent to look like Lena and that Lena herself had later collected the belongings at the B&B. Had Lena murdered her to give the impression that she herself had been murdered? If that was the case then the fact that she had collected her belongings afterwards did not make any sense. Had the woman been murdered in error and Lena had to try and remove any evidence of her being here? Had the murder anything to do with the army comrades? If Lena had committed the crime had she also killed Colm? They doubted if a woman would have had the strength to strangle a man as strong as Colm. What a strange case this was turning out to be. Calling to the B&B the DI told the owner that he would like to see the room that Lena had stayed in as even at this late stage he thought there might be something of interest there. Mrs O'Meara said that as it was not the tourist season no one else had been in the room. His main concern was to see if she had noticed any difference in Lena between her first and second visit. He asked her, "What was Lena like, was she jolly or quiet. Did she wear nice clothes? Did she seem worried or under stress? Did you notice any difference in her when she came to collect her things? Mrs O' Meara did not know what to make of all these questions and sat on the side of the bed before replying. "She did not say a whole lot but as she ate the meals I gave her I would not think she was under any type of stress. Her clothes were plain but fashionable and she wore no jewellery except for a gold chain around her neck." She looked the same when she returned for her things but I felt that she had forgotten to use makeup to cover her birthmark which I could see much clearer. There was nothing of interest in the room and as he had achieved his objective of learning about Lena's visits he thanked Mrs O'Meara and made his way back to the station. There seemed to be little doubt now that both Lena's had been to the B&B, the question was why? What was it that brought the murdered woman to the area? Was it, as her brother told them, to look for Lena's husband? Why did Lena herself not come? That she was to have a procedure on her birthmark did not stand up as it was obviously still there when she came to the B&B. How could she look for Lena's husband and at the same time not go to a hotel or to the shops? It did not make any sense and the DI believed that they would have to explore other avenues of enquiry. Jack felt that Lena had tried to use her friend as an alibi to disguise the fact that she was doing something elsewhere and it had all gone wrong. What, he thought, if she had actually needed to find her husband would she, in her depressed state, have thought up some elaborate scheme which failed. Her brother revealed that Lena had planned to meet his sister at the B&B and Jack wondered had Lena been here all the time? Mrs O'Meara would have told them if she had seen the two of them together so perhaps he could rule that theory out. What then was the reason for her being at the B&B and maybe more importantly who knew that she was there? Who was the person claiming to be a relative in the bar that had her picked up and brought to the vacant house? Did that person think it was Lena and for some reason became frightened? Would somebody have seen her arriving and spread the word? Had her husband thought she was there and if so would it have caused him to worry? Thinking of her, being brought to the café following a call from Joe Goode, he remembered Joe telling them that Lena had called to his cottage some time previous and wondered if he had thought that this woman was her. Jack asked the DI had Joe said anything about seeing Lena or had he just referred to her as the woman who he had rung for a taxi to pick her up. Once again marvelling at how Jack came up of these things he thought that this might be his new avenue of investigation. If Joe thought that he had recognised her would he have wondered why she had not known him? Would he have contacted her husband before ringing for a taxi?

That he had rung the casino, looking for a taxi, would that indicate her whereabouts would have been known by Kevin Burke and would it have given him reason to panic? The DI had never understood why Kevin had sent Jim and not a taxi to pick her up and thought he might now learn the truth. Joe could not believe that the DI and DS were once again knocking on his door and wondered what they would be looking for this time. "Joe" the DI said, "that woman who called and requested you to order a taxi did you recognise her?" Joe, looking a little sheepish, said, "That day I was not feeling too good and was lying down when I heard the knock on my door. Not expecting anybody to call I almost did not bother to answer it. I went to the door to see a woman with a case standing there but not having my glasses on I was not really able to see her very well. I remember having to put my reading glasses on to make the phone call but would have taken them off as other than for close up things I could not use them. My other ones where in my bedroom but I never went for them." He then heard the DI ask, "Did you think it strange that Jim Mescal and not a taxi called to collect her." Answering him Joe said, "well you see there was a bit of confusion as Jim thought he had been sent to bring me to the post office and he was not sure if he should take the woman. I told you earlier that I had not recognised her but I did get the impression that Jim may have thought that he had." What a shambles thought the DI as he wondered who he could believe. How would Jim react to being asked about his involvement in all of this. What about Denis who had collected her from the B&B and taken her to the empty house. Would he have any memories of that day? Would he be able to give a description of the customer, who claiming to be a relative, had asked him to pick her up. Jack wondered if when Denis had arrived at the B&B did the woman have a case ready which might indicate that she knew in advance that she was being picked up. He had never before experienced a case with so many twists and turns or with so many unanswered questions. They returned to the station to assess their latest information and decide what to do next. They all agreed that it was an unusual situation as most murder cases in the past had been straight forward with them knowing the identity of the victims and having clues or fingerprints leading them to finding the killers. This one was causing them some grief as there seemed to be no end to the possibilities surrounding both murders. They found it hard to understand that there could be a connection between an unknown woman and Colm, the other victim, and wondered if either of them involved the army comrades. The only conclusion, that they could see as believable, was that the woman had been mistaken for Lena and there had to have been some previous interaction between Lena and the army comrades. The talk of them having some type of pact gave rise to think that perhaps one of the group had threatened to break their silence and had to be punished. The question being asked was who was supposed to receive this punishment and did it require a murder and perhaps a second killing? The super felt that the answers all hinged around whether or not Lena was the intended victim and the woman's murder was an error or that she had been murdered with no thoughts of her being part of any pact. The idea of a vow of silence had never been fully verified and they wondered if it ever would be. "Where to next" they heard the super say and wondered the same themselves. The DI spoke next and said, "Would speaking to either Jim or Kevin bring anything new to light, they only other people connected to that group is Declan and Madge or Bert who I fear would not be much help to us." Jack asked if having a further conversation with Anthony and Betty Gleeson at the café would help. They would also have to talk to Denis and listen to what he had to say in relation to the customer who had asked him to pick up the murdered woman. Following another hour of discussion the DI finally said, "Firstly we will speak with Denis and try to establish the identity of the customer, failing that we will speak to Jim and see does he remember anything being said as he took her to the café that night. I doubt if we will learn anything new by speaking to Kevin but we will give it a try. Failing all this I will make another hospital visit and may be lucky to find Bert in better shape and ready to answer some questions. Declan and Madge, although part of the army group, do not seem to be very well informed about what is happening so I am doubtful of learning anything from them. That only leaves Anthony and Betty and if what they have told us is true they will not have much to add to our investigation." The super reminded them that it was getting late and thought that they could start their interviews first thing the following morning.

Jack was taking Charlotte to a show and was delighted to finally be getting out of the station. This case was taking far too much of his time and energy and he could not wait to relax and enjoy a night out. He was surprised not to see Charlotte at home as she usually finished a little earlier than him. He had a shower and had started preparing the dinner before Charlotte came in. Explaining that she had been delayed as she had spotted Luke walking towards the harbour with Kevin Burke the security guard from the casino and had shadowed them. She had been aware of his involvement in the kidnapping and wondered if he was hatching something new with Luke. They did not go aboard and she wondered why walk all that way if they had not intended sailing. They turned around and walked back in the direction of the casino. Jack became focused on this information and felt that if they were to interview him and he thought they were going to bring him in for questioning he might do as he had imagined and leave the country using Luke's yacht. He was sure that he did not just go to the harbour without a good reason. Charlotte now showered joined him for their meal and both agreed not to discuss work related items for the rest of the evening.

CHAPTER FORTY-THREE
Kevin Rows With Jim

Jim, who had not been in touch with Luke since missing out on the Amsterdam incident, also observed them going towards the yacht and wondered had Luke decided to start up again with a new partner. He had arranged to meet Kevin that evening and wondered would he be told anything about this new companion. He was due to meet him at Declan's place and there meeting was to do with their ongoing problem and with Declan and Madge present he would hardly say anything about the yacht. Nothing new emerged and there seemed to be a lot less tension between them. The one thing to which they all agreed was to maintain their silence no matter what happened. The atmosphere changed as soon as they left and started to walk towards their cars. Kevin became very aggressive and told Jim that he believed he had almost incriminated him in the murders. Jim was caught off guard as Kevin continued the onslaught and said, "If you are called in to the garda station again and I hear that you have uttered one word against me yours could be the next body found in the woods. You are only going to get one warning so make sure you remember it. We are the only two who know where you got that handbag so I will know who opened their mouth, very quickly, if I hear that anybody else gets to know of it. Another thing, I saw you following me earlier when I was with your friend, Luke, or should I say ex-friend, and again I do not want that spoken about. You and I go back a long time but that will not stop me dealing severely with you if I think you are double crossing me. We will remain friends, without anybody ever knowing we had this conversation, as long as you understand what I have just said." Jim was in a state of shock and just said that he understood and would not say a word to anybody. Inside he was seething, his unexpressed anger bubbling up inside him. Who did he think he was to speak down to him in this manner? If he was so afraid of what might be said against him perhaps he did have a lot to hide. Remain friends he had said, as and from this minute he has lost me as a friend and I will stay as far away from him as possible. As he reached his car Kevin turned and drawing his finger across his throat said, "Do not forget or you will be sorry." Kevin then went to work at the casino as if nothing had happened leaving Jim, in a terrible state, knowing that he would have to be very careful if he had any hope of avoiding serious conflict. Knowing that he had still to answer for the kidnapping in which Kevin was also involved he worried that he would have to include him during his court appearance and spent many sleepless nights trying to think of a way around it. It bothered him to think that Kevin had turned so vicious and he became convinced that there must be an underlying cause that he was not aware of. Could it be that he was involved in the murders? It seemed unlikely but something big had to be bothering him. Thinking of seeing him with Luke he wondered if he also knew Mark and could he have had anything to do with Gareth's death in Spain. He was glad that he had made his mind up to move and get a job once the business of the kidnapping was over.

Back in the shop Declan and Madge were feeling happy as they thought of how relaxed Kevin and Jim had been and hoped the murderer would be caught and they could all get back to a peaceful life again. Little did they know of the conversation that had taken place between Kevin and Jim.

On the other side of the town Jack and Charlotte, having spent an enjoyable few hours at the theatre followed by a few drinks at the bar, were heading to bed looking forward to another night of absolute bliss never thinking of the drama unfolding around them.

CHAPTER FORTY-FOUR
Denis and Jim Nervous

Going to see Denis the following morning the DI had no idea where he was going to start. Is main focus was to find out who the customer was but thought it best not to begin with such a direct question. They met Denis in the bar and as there were no customers he had the time to speak to them. Jack asked him if he remembered what the lady was wearing, which seemed to confuse him, and did she have any jewellery. He said that he had not taken any notice of her clothes and did not know if she was wearing jewellery. The DI then asked him "Was she surprised when you called or was she waiting for you?" "She was taken aback and did not want to come with me but Mrs O'Meara told her I only lived down the road and it was alright to go with me. When she heard that a relative was looking for her to stay with him she got her case and came out to the car." "Denis" he heard the DI say, "Who was this customer who asked you to collect her, was he a regular?" He was just about to answer when Kevin Burke interrupted them by saying that there was a phone call for him. Saying that he would not be long he went out to the phone which was in the lobby. The DI could not see what transpired but when Denis came back in he told them that he had never seen the customer before. Had they been in a position to observe the lobby they would have seen Kevin chastising Denis and warning him not to say anymore or he would end up, like Bert, in hospital. Denis, having witnessed Kevin dealing with awkward customers, knew better than to argue and did exactly what was expected of him. Jack was annoyed at not getting the information and wondered who could have known that Denis was being interviewed and phoned him. He did not realise that it was Kevin who had caused the interruption. The DI had watched Kevin closely and was convinced that it was him who had warned Denis not to say anymore. Thinking to himself, he thought that he must ensure that Denis was alone before speaking to him again. Why had Kevin not wanted them to find out who the customer was? Was he a friend or was Kevin covering for himself? Whatever it was that bound these army comrades together was certainly holding up the investigation.

Jim Mescal was next on their list and not knowing what had happened between him and Kevin, they were quite unprepared for the reception they received. They had asked to meet him in the café but he declined and asked for the interview to be held in the station. Watching his furtive approach they knew that something had happened and wondered what it could have been. Asking him about collecting the woman and bringing her to the café brought about a very hostile reaction and he denied speaking to her. "Why are you asking me all these questions again? I thought I had told you everything that you needed to know. "You told us that you came to pick up Joe Goode and bring him to the post office but you never explained why you changed your mind and took this woman to the café instead." "Does it make all that much difference now" he said and added "Joe insisted that he had rung for a taxi for her and as I had come instead I should take her back into town." Asking him again about his conversation Jim reiterated that they had not had one and said that the only thing she had asked was to bring her to the cafe. "Have you any idea, as she had not been out of the B&B, how she knew about the café." Jim, thinking of the warning that he had been given, made sure that he said nothing that might incriminate Kevin. Replying he just said, "I have no idea about her stay in the B&B but the café was where she wanted to go." Two interviews, and they were still no better off. The one change that the DI noticed was the high level of tension in both Denis and Jim and wondered if they had anything to do with the murders. He would have liked to interview Kevin but other than the casino key found at the murder site, which he did not wish Kevin to know about yet, he had nothing to tie him to anything related to the murder. Denis saw Jim coming out of the station and wondered what he had been doing there. He crossed the road to meet him and they went to the café for a coffee. Their conversation was subdued as they both refrained from mentioning the threats they had received. Not being busy Declan got a coffee and joined them hoping to get an update. He asked Jim did he think that the get together had gone well and told them he was pleased that everyone had finally begun to realise that the murders had nothing to do with any of them and where now more relaxed. Jim agreed that he had enjoyed the evening, but with thoughts of Kevin's threats fresh in his mind he did not elaborate in case he said something out of place. Declan, trying not to sound inquisitive, asked had Kevin been to see Bert recently saying that he had forgotten to ask him on the evening of the get together. As neither of them felt like speaking about Kevin they both replied that they had not heard anything. I was wondering if they would let me in to see him as, up to now, it has not been possible to get away from here. Again they just answered that they did not know. Marge had been watching them and with feminine intuition knew that they were deliberately avoiding saying anything that could be interpreted incorrectly. She was a little confused as she had felt that Jim had been in much better form when he was there the previous evening. Denis had not been there and she thought there could be some tension between Jim and himself. Strange she thought, as she listened to their conversation and realised that the tension was not between them but shared by them against somebody else. With no customers to look after she joined them thinking that she might learn what it was that was bothering them. She asked Jim did he and Kevin have the same solicitor representing them for the kidnap case and knew by his demeanour, before he even spoke, that he did not want to answer that question. Sorry Marge but at the moment I do not have an answer for you as I do not know myself yet. She knew by the look that passed between Denis and Jim that she had hit on something that had affected them both. She had never seen them together in the café before and this got her thinking that perhaps that they had both had a row with the same person and were commiserating with each other. She wondered could it have been Kevin or perhaps Mark and as she knew both of them could be dangerous she decided not to ask any more questions. Herself and Declan went into their living space and left them to finish their coffee. Retreating inside Madge asked Declan what he thought of Jim's changed attitude and all she heard was "what changed attitude I never noticed anything." Jim wondering what the questions were all about worried that Kevin had told them about the statement he had almost signed and they were just trying to have him confirm his story. Denis, not really knowing Declan or Marge just thought they were only making small talk as he would do behind the bar if he was not busy. On their own Denis asked him had he been called to the Garda station again in connection with the kidnapping or the handbags. "Have you been talking to Kevin? Did he say anything about the handbags to you? Has he upset you also?" Denis was quick to notice the 'also' and knew that they had both had a warning in some form or another. "Jim I think it's time for us to level with each other, we may need to stand up for ourselves very soon and together we may have a better chance of succeeding if we pull together." They each told of their experience with Kevin and agreed that it would be better if they were not seen together except in the bar where Kevin would expect them to be. They agreed that they would not allow him to get away with this form of behaviour but as yet did not know what action they could take. Jim knew that it would always be possible for him to implicate him further with the kidnapping as he had only not done so to avoid himself getting into more trouble. Denis was also thinking of what evidence he could use against him if he threatened him again.

Kevin, back at work, was conscious of having annoyed both Jim and Denis but did not think that either of them presented a threat to him. He would just have to keep the pressure on them and keep them from speaking to anyone about his involvement in anything. Forming an alliance with Luke was his method of preparing his escape as he had no intention of going to prison if he could help it. He had heard about Gareth's deception and used this knowledge to convince Luke of a way for them to get their hands on a lot of money. Luke, still vulnerable following his big loss, could not resist Kevin's offer and never doubted him for a moment. Kevin capitalised on being aware of the lobster pot idea and used it to fire up Luke's imagination. He would go out into the open sea with Luke and learn how to handle the yacht and when the time was right he would sail off leaving not a trace and avoid a prison sentence. He now had to create a viable money-making venture and convince Luke of its merits. He wondered if Mark would have any ideas or would be interested in joining him. On hearing what Kevin had in mind Mark, also needing to know that he could vanish if needed, told Kevin that he was interested as long as Luke did not know. What a combination, Mark with lots of contacts, Luke with clever ideas, thought up mainly by Margaret, and Kevin with his military training, what could go wrong? The casino could not be used so it was decided to use the yacht for their meetings. Mark, the unknown to Luke partner, would not attend but would be briefed by Kevin and his ideas put into the discussions as part of Kevin's contribution. If this all worked out Kevin would make some money, not go to prison and find himself a new home far away before he was missed.

CHAPTER FORTY-FIVE
Building Up The Evidence

The investigation had grinded to a halt and the team were beginning to wonder if a break would ever come. The super had thought with the finding of the casino key they would have been able to arrest Kevin but the DI reminded her that it was Jim's fingerprints on the bank card and this would have given Kevin's solicitor a field day and the evidence of the key would have been thrown out of court. He knew he had to accumulate a more substantial case before attempting to arrest anybody for the murder or murders. That no evidence was available for either murder led him to believe that they were connected and if he could just link them together he may be on his way to solving both of them. In consultation with the super and the DS it was agreed to take a step back and each of them to consider just one scenario.

Jack thought that he would follow the idea that an unknown woman had been murdered and Mark who had seen it happen was silenced by the murderer. So started his side of the investigation.

The DI had other ideas. It was his belief that she had been mistaken for Lena and he felt if he concentrated on finding her killer Colm's death may become apparent. The super's role would be to correlate their findings and point out similarities. The DI started by listing the facts as he knew them. Jim's fingerprints found on her bank cards; Kevin's casino room key found at Colm's murder site. The murder victim having purple substance on her face giving him the impression that it had been done to replicate a birthmark similar to that on Lena's face. Lena had been part of an army group of whom two had been murdered and another one lay in hospital following a shooting accident. Following his theory that it was Lena, not the murdered woman, who was the intended victim he needed to work out who felt that she should be murdered, who was in a position to murder her and what would have been the motive for her murder. Alternatively had she just been the victim of a random attack with no reason other than she happened to be in the wrong place at the wrong time. Putting motive first he had to put Lena's husband in the frame if only because, he was in the area and after ten years, he had felt the need to see her body. If he had thought that he had killed her and then heard that she was still alive would he have just come to see who it was that he had murdered by mistake? That she had been in the army the DI would have to consider the remaining members of that group who served with her. That included Bert, Kevin, Jim, Declan, Madge and perhaps someone else from that group yet unknown to him. He also had to keep an open mind as to the possibility that any one that he knew to have been in the forest could be responsible. Any one of those could have been in a position to commit the crime. Was there an underlying reason for someone wishing to see her dead? Had she witnessed an incident and was perhaps blackmailing someone? Was it a case that somebody felt that she was a threat or there was a chance that, in her mental state, she might reveal some information that could be embarrassing or even detrimental? That Gareth, another of the army comrades, had been murdered in Spain, allegedly in connection with a diamond robbery, gave him food for thought and he wondered could it also have been connected. He had a meeting with the super and discussed what the best avenue of investigation may be.

Jack was starting out on his quest to find the murderer. He hoped that by helping to solve this crime it would improve his chances of promotion in the future. Walking around the murder site in the forest, where he thought he might get some inspiration, he remembered that Colm had been strangled and believed that a man not a woman was responsible. If he could identify him then he would probably have both murders solved. Who could he consider from those he knew where there over that weekend? Patrick and Michael Jones, Anthony Gleeson and Declan O'Grady. John Oliver and George Palmer had also been out walking. Knowing the DI had the army comrades on his list he decided not to waste time thinking about them. Could a robbery have gone terribly wrong for Denis, the one person who he had not heard of being in the forest but who was involved with stealing handbags? Would he have been strong enough to strangle Colm? Had he been operating with Jim and had he murdered him? It suddenly dawned on him that Jim was in custody at the time of Colm's death and he realised that he would have to slow down and think more clearly. From their interviews he was convinced that no one else had been in the hills during the day so would he have to consider that it had occurred during the night? Had they any evidence that the forest had been used outside of the usual daylight hours. Mr Goode had said he saw two people going towards the car park while it was still dark and he remembered Anthony Gleeson admitting that he had gone out walking early on Sunday morning but would he have had the time to commit a murder and meet Amelia as well. By mid-day he was beginning to think that the DI was more likely on the right track and at the afternoon meeting he suggested joining him and continuing the investigation together.

Both super and DI agreed and thought with 'the team' back together they might finally get a break. The super suggested visiting Bert again and if he had recovered a little perhaps he could enlighten them as to the army comrades past behaviour. She had relied in the past on her gut feeling and felt that both murders revolved around Lena and her army comrades. Knowing the super's past record they took her advice and made an appointment to go to the hospital. Seeing him the DI thought he had improved but he still gave the impression of having no memory and was unable to enlighten then in any way. The DI unconvinced made an appointment to speak with his doctor and learned that it was believed that Bert was in a much better place than he admitted to. His brain scans showed almost normal activity and they thought that it suited him to give the impression of not being able to remember anything. He asked the doctor what would happen if Bert continued with a loss of memory and was told that, as the accident happened while on duty, he would get early retirement and possibly compensation to provide for whatever after care he would need. There would be very little chance of him ever going to court on the kidnapping or a murder charge. They returned to the incident room and added this knowledge to their notice board. Should they consider Gareth's murder as being part of this circle. The international division knew of Mark's involvement with Gareth and the diamond smuggling but had he connections with the army comrades? Jack suggested speaking to Declan and Madge and asking them about Mark. They both denied knowing him but remarked that Gareth would have been a friend. Declan said, "He was never in the army but got to know Gareth through the charity group. We believe he went to join Gareth in Spain before he was murdered." Once again the DI believed that he was not being told the truth and wondered why they all denied knowing each other.

CHAPTER FORTY-SIX

Kevin and Mark Conspiring

Kevin became the centre of their attention as they watched him regularly going to the yacht. A pattern seemed to be emerging as on the days he went to the yacht Mark inevitably met him afterwards at the casino. It certainly looked as if something was being planned. Could these meetings be connected to what had happened or could they expect something new to occur in the future. It was a strange set up to understand. They knew Luke and Mark had been together in the charity group and they had both been in Spain at the time around Gareth's murder and yet now Luke did not seem to have any idea that Mark was in league with Kevin in whatever was going on between them. Would Jack be right when he suggested that Kevin was preparing an escape route for himself should he need it. It may soon be necessary to keep a closer eye on the harbour and have the Garda launch standing by. The super thought they should go to the casino and have a chat with Denis at the bar on the evening they knew that Mark would be there and see if there was any reaction. Making it look as if they had come to see Denis they came into the bar as Mark was arriving. A look of consternation on Kevin's face said it all as he ushered Mark out of the bar and into a side room. Denis was equally disturbed by their presence or was it due to knowing that Kevin had seen him speaking to the DI. Denis tried hard to hide his feelings but when Kevin walked up to the bar he turned positively pale. Kevin never said a word but his presence was enough to terrify Denis. He asked the DI did he wish to speak to him to which the DI replied " No, not this evening Denis, we were just passing and thought we would have a coffee before heading back to the station." Deliberately sitting where they could observe Mark coming back out they drank their coffee and relaxed knowing that they had caused some concern to a few people. Mark never did reappear so they assumed he had been shown another way out avoiding any further embarrassment. The super hearing of the reaction said that they should do it more often and rattle a few feathers. Perhaps if Denis is put under enough pressure he may open up and assist us. The DI thought it was Jim that would need to speak out but knew that at this point in time he was too scared.

CHAPTER FORTY-SEVEN
Bert Recovers

Getting a call from Commandant Harris asking him to call in to see him was unexpected but he lost no time in heading over to the barracks. A huge surprise awaited him; one he had never expected. Sitting in the commandant's office was Bert Delaney, in full uniform and although not looking well was certainly a lot better than the last time he had seen him. He stood up and shaking the DI's hand said he needed to have a conversation with him. He told of how he had organised the kidnapping but had since met with Lucy and agreed to grant her a divorce as a way of making up for all the stress he had caused her. Sha said that she would not press charges and he hoped that the DI would not do so either. Before he had a chance to answer Bert said, "I believe some of my friends have lost their lives recently and in return for you not bringing me to court I will assist you in any way I can to bring whoever is responsible to justice. My memory has not returned completely but I am hopeful that it will be sufficient to be able to understand and answer your questions. While formulating a reply the DI heard Commandant Harris say, "Sergeant Major Delaney, up to the time of his injury, was a highly respected and competent soldier. His action was brought about by the thoughts of losing his wife and as he has unreservedly apologised to her and has settled the matter to her satisfaction we would appreciate you doing whatever you can to help him. He would be a great loss to us if we were to lose him." In answering they heard the DI say, "I have to make a few things clear, firstly it would not be up to me to say that you will or will not be charged with the kidnapping. Yes, if I consider it is a reasonable request, I can put in a recommendation to that effect. I, must at this time, tell you that as you may well have been in the forest at the time of the first murder you are on our list of suspects even though we feel that both murders are connected and we are aware that you could not have been involved in the second one. One more thing I would like to point out to you, withholding information in a murder investigation is a very serious offence and in itself could lead to imprisonment. Before we continue can I be assured that you understand all that I have said and you are still willing to co-operate in our attempt to find the perpetrators of these horrific crimes." Bert getting a very obvious nod from his CO said, "Yes Sir, I fully understand and as I am also determined to have my friend's murderer found I will give every assistance I can." Turning to the CO the DI asked him to arrange a solicitor for Bert and said that he would be happy to conduct the interview at the barracks but could not promise what the outcome would be and he may have to take Bert into custody at some stage. The DI, on his return to the station, decided to check with Lucy that what Bert had told him was true. By now she was back in the city but he had no trouble locating her. She confirmed Bert's story and said that it was so strange meeting him, she added that he had been almost like the man she had first met and instead of using the bullying tactics as he had after they parted, he was gentle and even considerate. For a moment, the DI thought she was going to say that she was considering living with him again. Before she hung up she said, "I will be coming down to that hotel again for a few days when the divorce is completed and I hope it will be possible for us to have a coffee together." He agreed to do that and wondered would she be seeing Michael Jones and doing some hill walking again. Thinking back to Bert he wondered what information he could get from him that would help to close this case. Learning what thoughts he had on his own accident could be enlightening? Did he consider that it was anything but an accident? Was that the reason why he wanted to help with the investigation? Would he have any idea why one of the comrades might have wished to murder Lena and had killed the wrong person? Would he be aware of anyone who would have been capable of committing murder? The DI was conscious that he must remember that Bert was still on his list of suspects for the first murder and would have to analyse any information he received from him. Would Bert, having been the best man at Lena's wedding, have kept in touch and would he know where she was living?

Just As he finished writing his notes Jack told him that he had found some interesting items relating to Margaret Simpson, Luke's fiancée. As the DI had not seen her mentioned at any time in connection with the murders he was surprised that Jack had been looking for information on her. "What put you to thinking that she might help us?" Jack laughed and explained that he had not been investigating her but looking on line to price a diamond ring when he noticed a reference to her pricing diamonds. I skipped by her enquiry but saw another one where she was asking for continental wholesale outlets and that started me thinking of what had happened to Gareth in Amsterdam. She had received a number of replies some of which seemed to be worded strangely and at first I took it to be the language interpretation. I checked out a few of the numbers and soon realised they were not what they seemed to be. As soon as I started making genuine enquires about their sales I was transferred to a different number and I am sure that there must be a code or password needed to access these places. "My thoughts were that if Luke was planning to buy diamonds again and Kevin was caught up in it was there a chance that he would use this opportunity to vanish and not have to face the kidnapping charge? Knowing that Luke is unaware of Mark being involved makes me wonder if he and Kevin are making plans of their own with a view to hijacking the yacht for themselves?" The DI, with his thoughts more on interviewing Bert, just said that they would watch the yacht and wait for developments.

CHAPTER FORTY-EIGHT

Bert Reveals Old Secrets

The DI asked Jack to accompany him to the barracks where in the presence of Bert's solicitor they conducted the interview. They learned that Lena's brother had not gone missing but had died in a hunting accident in which all the army comrades were involved. The panicked and instead of reporting it they buried him and swore a vow of secrecy. He told them that Alfonsi Nowak, Lena's cousin, had advised them that they would all be jailed if his death was reported. I was the only one who had seen Alfonsi fire the gun that killed him but being in a foreign country I was afraid to say anything. Over the years the memory haunted me and I could sympathise with Lena having her breakdowns. There never seemed to be any reason to change our position and up until the murder everything continued to be all right. I had not heard from her and except for the few visits we never kept in touch. Her husband, although they had split up shortly after the wedding, worried about her health and kept in touch with me. He thought that she might look for help and asked me to let him know if she did. That never happened and I did not know that she had come over until I heard of the murder. I do not understand how another person with the same name got caught up in everything. I do not think the murders were orchestrated by Lena even in her depressed state. Her husband Antoni cared for her even if it was at a distance and would certainly not have done anything to harm her. The DI concluded the interview by advising Bert's solicitor that he could remain at the barracks but could not travel without his permission. This was agreed and the DI headed back towards the station. Both he and Jack felt that what they had been told sounded like the truth and they thought that it would not be long before they could arrest the person responsible for the murders.

On their way back Jack spotted Kevin, carrying a large backpack, heading in the direction of the yacht and was curious to know what he had in it. Not being in a position to stop and ask him he had to let it go. Some times in this life you can get lucky and for Jack this was one of those days. His friend William was relaxing fishing off the pier and saw Kevin, who he knew from the casino, removing part of a lobster pot from his bag and leaving it on board the yacht. Yachts were not usually used for this type of fishing and he wondered what it was for. As it was only a part he thought that he was needing to repair one and would not have thought of it again if he had not remembered Jack explaining about the idea of using a lobster pot to conceal and deliver diamonds. He knew Jack was watching Kevin and quickly told him what he had seen. This got the DI's attention and he arranged for a watch to be maintained on the yacht. It soon became apparent that something was being set up as more parts were put on board and a complete cage assembled. Luke still did not seem to realise that Mark was part of the plans which left Jack wondering what was being planned and by who? Margaret had not been seen so it was thought that she must be operating from the cottage. With evidence building up it was getting more important each day that they learned what was happening and make arrangements to prevent it. They had no evidence to show any form of deception but somehow knowing the individuals concerned it was most likely that something underhand was brewing. The yacht sailed out each morning and the Gardai watching it could see that Kevin was learning how to handle it. Being motorised there was no need to hoist the sails and he seemed to pick up the rudiments of sailing quickly. Watching the journeys lengthen as the days went by the DI got a little apprehensive and knew that they would have to get all the evidence needed to pick up Kevin before he sailed away completely. They now knew that he had been instrumental in the death and cover up of Lena's brother and they were sure that the key found at the murder belonged to him. They needed a statement from Jim confirming who had given him the handbag to feel that they had enough evidence to arrest him. What could be done to take the pressure of Jim and allow him to give them what they needed. While the DI was trying to come up with a solution he received a message telling him that Mark had gone aboard the yacht for the first time and was heading out into the bay. Neither Luke nor Kevin seemed to be on board and everyone wondered what was going on. The Garda launch was ready to sail but not wanting to alert Mark waited to see how far he would go. The yacht did a few circles of the bay and returned to the quay wall and tied up. Mark came ashore leaving everybody undecided as to what he might have been doing. Jack thought that he had been doing a dummy trip to see if any notice had been taken of him. It was confusing to see him on his own especially as they knew that Luke did not even know he was involved with the scheme. Was he thinking of going it alone and taking the yacht without Luke or Kevin being consulted? The super thought it would suit her plans if that happened as it would remove the necessity of watching the yacht as a way of escape for Kevin. Another morning another meeting as they tried to come up with some way of proving that Kevin was the one they were looking for. All the evidence so far pointed in his direction but unless they had a watertight case they would never be able to bring charges against him. New evidence came from a source that they never expected as a phone call from Joe Goode was received asking the DI to visit him right away. The DI left the meeting and drove out to Joe's cottage where he found him in a very nervous state. He told the DI that he had not been truthful when talking about the couple he had seen going into the forest but he had never considered that it had anything to do with the murder. He said that on the day that Colm had been murdered the same person had gone into the forest with him but returned on his own. He had not realised how important it could be until he heard of Colm's death. He was terrified that he could be blamed as he had not told the truth and had said nothing. The DI asked him if he knew who it was would he tell him now. Still nervous he said," It was Kevin Burke from the casino." The DI not fully believing him asked "What changed your mind and made you feel you had to speak up now." Replying Joe said, "I got a call from Antoni who said that if I wanted to help his wife I should tell you everything. I did not understand what difference it would make to her but I was sure he would not have rung me if he had not thought it important." "Mr Goode you need to sign a statement confirming what you have just told me so we will go to the station now." Joe surprised him by handing him a statement and agreed to sign it so that he would know the signature was genuine. "One last thing before you go can you promise that he will not know that I gave you this before you have him arrested and safely in jail." "You have my word on that and if for any reason he is released I will arrange protection for you." The Di returned to the incident room and showed the statement to the super who was delighted at the thought of having one more item of importance to hold against Kevin. What was it that kept holding her back from having him brought in and questioned again? Part of her was sure that he was who they were looking for but always that doubt remained preventing her from arresting him in case she was wrong. She knew that she could stall until she had everything she wanted as he could not go anywhere without his passport. Saying this Jack reminded her that if he sailed away on the yacht he could easily buy a false passport and he would be very hard to find. The following morning she got a report advising her that the yacht was nowhere to be seen and must have sailed out under the cover of darkness. Believing it would reappear later she settled down to checking all the facts surrounding the case and seeing what evidence she could use with safety. Seeing Kevin walking along the main street she assumed the yacht had returned and could not believe it when he actually came into the station to report it missing. He said that Luke had come down to the harbour to go out for fuel but it was not on the berth when he arrived. He said that is first thoughts were that he had decided to get a practice run around the bay but on ringing me he realised that I was at work in the casino. The super asked him had he any idea who may have taken it. She knew that it would be difficult for him to answer that as even if he knew that Mark had it he would not be able to say anything. That Luke did not even know about Mark being in the circle must have been worrying for him. All he said was that he had no idea but knowing that there was very little fuel in it he thought that whoever it was could not go too far. She said that she would hand it over to the harbour police and she was sure that they would make a thorough search. She began to wonder if he had been involved with the murders would he have just been able to walk calmly into the station and report a missing yacht. She thought how easy one single incident can begin to put doubts into your brain and cause you to change your timing of your pre-set plan. She thought it would have been Luke the owner of the yacht who should have reported it missing. No time for worrying about a yacht but it was a small comfort to know that Kevin could not use it unless it was recovered. She advised Kevin that she would keep him updated if she learned anything. A rather dejected Mr Burke left the station and headed back in the direction of the harbour probably hoping to see the yacht back in its place. He had not been able to contact Mark but found it hard to believe that he would have sailed away without him. He reasoned that as neither of them had enough money to start a new life there would have been very little point in him going off anywhere. A thought that perhaps he had been scheming on his own worried him a little but he shrugged it off and headed back towards the casino. He just had to hope that if it was him that he had only gone on a trial run to make sure he remembered how to sail it. Although he knew they had planned to take it he was not yet in a position to do so as he needed to organise a new passport and get some cash together. He had convinced Luke that his scheme would bring in enough cash for them both but had no intention of sharing it with him. Things had been progressing nicely but if the yacht was missing then all his effort would have been in vain. That he was able to walk in and out of the Garda station gave him a false sense of security as he believed if they had evidence against him thy would have arrested him then. This he believed gave him a longer time frame before he would eventually have to flee. His thoughts turned to Jim and he wondered would he have been the one to have taken the yacht in retaliation for him warning him about telling tales. That sounded far more logical than Mark having any part of it. As he got close to the casino he rang Jim but got no reply. He was now convinced that Jim, knowing that he was involved with Luke, had probably guessed what he had in mind and was determined to prevent him leaving. He got to thinking that Denis was also involved in the plan and swore, without any evidence of it being true, to punish both of them as soon as they returned. Luke was stunned that somebody had taken his yacht but knowing it contained very little fuel felt it would be put ashore very quickly and he would be able to pick it up. He waited patiently to hear of it being found until he looked at his bank balance and saw that €200 had been spent at the filling barge where he normally bought his fuel. Whoever had taken the yacht obviously knew where he kept his credit card and somehow had access to his security code. Driving down to the barge he was told that two men had pulled alongside and had filled up. They had paid in the normal way so he had not seen anything wrong. Relating this to Kevin it seemed certain that Jim and Denis were responsible. Now the question was where would they have put it. Denis arriving in to work was accosted by Kevin demanding to know where he and Jim had left the yacht. Denis, not even knowing that the yacht was missing, was dumfounded and proclaimed his innocence. He tried to explain that Jim had gone to the hospital for an appointment but it fell on deaf ears with Kevin totally out of control. Had the manager not appeared Denis would most certainly have felt Kevin's anger expressed in violence. The manager calmed things a little and told Kevin that Denis had been working from early that morning and was only coming back from his lunch. As they spoke Jim came into the bar, with a surgical dressing across his cheek, having had a small procedure to remove a growth on his face. Keven had himself so worked up thinking that they had been involved that he found it impossible to believe that they had not. If not them, then who? Must he consider Mark again now perhaps with an accomplice? He was completely confused but trying to hold himself together he retreated into the security room only to be faced by Mark who was waiting for an update on the morning meeting. He had noticed that the yacht was not in its usual place and thought they had decided to hold their meeting in the bay. That Mark had not been involved was a great relief but left them wondering who had taken it. In the meantime Luke had seen camera footage as the fuel had been pumped aboard but both men had very cleverly kept out of the camera range. It was very frustrating and he accepted that he might never see the yacht again. Kevin still thinking of acquiring an escape plan thought that if Bert had recovered he may be able to help him. Ringing the hospital he was advised that Bert had been discharged and was convalescing somewhere in the country. He never doubted this nor realised that Bert had asked that this message be given to anybody looking for him. His only ally left was Declan and other than sheltering him in their house there was little they could do for him. Could he trust Mark? Would he be able to arrange a quick departure if needed? Would the yacht turn up and if it did would it ever be left unlocked again? He thought that the best thing for him to do was to stay at work until he could think of a way out of his troubles. He had not realised that as he had left the Garda station the super had rung her friend in the harbour police and asked him if they did find the yacht to secure it elsewhere and not say it had been found. She explained that she needed a few more days to tie up a murder case and as the main suspect had access to the yacht she was afraid that he might vanish before he was arrested. He laughed as he said that if it ever turned up he would be surprised but of course he could arrange that for her. As she finished the conversation the DI reminded her of the statement he had received from Mr Goode and suggested picking Kevin up for questioning. She maintained that she needed proof of his involvement with the hand bag that Jim had dumped and gave him instructions to arrest Jim instead. She was determined to get the truth regarding the handbag which she felt could be the key to unlocking this tiresome case. She had him brought to the station but he refused to say a word without his solicitor being present. The DI observing him felt that he was actually terrified and had to consider that he had been threatened. As far as he was aware the only other person involved, as almost confessed by Jim, was Kevin Burke. What could he be holding over Jim to cause such fear? Did Jim do something in the past that Kevin knew about? Had Jim been, apart from the handbag incident, involved with something recently that Kevin had been aware of? With Jim so afraid there was very little hope of getting any information from him until he calmed down. His solicitor, also aware of his fear, was not at all happy that his client had been put under this type of pressure. He requested a private few minutes and spoke to him in relation to him being threatened. Jim explained that it was not the DI who had built up the pressure but he could not say who it was. Jim, more afraid of Kevin than the law, denied being nervous and said he was worried that they would blame him for the murder which he had nothing to do with. Listening to his solicitor he heard him say, "Jim, you may not have been involved but the fact remains that your fingerprints are on that woman's card. The DI would have every right to hold you here even if he believes you did not commit the crime yourself. I advised you, the last time we spoke, not to sign a statement but if that same person has you in this state I have to change my thinking and assume that he may have been involved with the murder. If it is him who has threatened you, and I do believe you have been threatened, you will have to consider whether you want to be accused of withholding information, a serious offence in a murder case, or facing a lifetime of running away from this person." The solicitor indicated that he was now ready to return to the interview room and with a very shaken and unsure Jim he joined the super an DI. During the course of the next few hours his spirit broke and with the help of his solicitor made a deal with the super. He emphasized that he did not know if Kevin had anything to do with the murder, all he was sure of was that he had been given the handbag by him to dump. He agreed to sign a statement naming Kevin as long as he could remain safe in custody until Kevin had been arrested and charged with the murder. He was advised that if Kevin was charged and did not admit to doing it that his solicitor could look for bail and it was possible that he would be out on the streets again. Jim's solicitor then asked the DI if, in return for a signed statement, he would drop the kidnap charges and allow Jim to move away to a spot where Kevin would not find him. This compromise was agreed by the super and the statement was signed.

Kevin was arrested and when told that they knew what had happened to Lena's brother, told that there was a witness who would swear that he had been seen going into the forest at the time of the murders, shown the key which had been found by Colm's body and Jim's statement was revealed he confessed to both murders. He told them that on hearing that Lena was staying at the B&B, without having told them as she had always done previously, he had received a shock. Why would she be visiting after all this time? The last he had heard of her was that she was having another breakdown and with this in mind he had become concerned that she may have come seeking revenge for the death of her brother Tobias. He believed that she knew that he was the one that fired the shot that had killed him and had come to get her revenge. He arranged for Denis to bring her on a wild goose chase and then had her brought to the café. Before he had time to work it all out he had collected her, from the café, early the following morning and telling her that she could see a beautiful sunrise from the forest track, had taken her into the forest where he had murdered her. She was a lot different from when he had last seen her but he had put that down to the early morning start. He had been a little confused when she did not seem to recognise him or hold any type of conversation with him but he had never doubted that it was her. He was horrified to learn that it was not the Lena he believed her to be and found it hard to cope with that. Being caught up in the kidnapping and not in a position to travel anywhere complicated everything and he had hoped that his mistake would not be discovered. He still feared that Jim, under pressure, might tell of receiving the hand bag to dump, from him and was urgently trying to find a way of explaining how he had got it if he was questioned. Receiving a call from Colm O'Hara asking him to meet in the carpark started alarm bells ringing as he wondered what it was that he wanted to speak to him about. He was not long learning that Colm, who had also been concerned on realising that Lena was close by, had gone out early to think things through and had seen him going to the forest with her. With thoughts in his head, that they were planning something together, he had followed them and was horrified to see him killing her. He had believed, at the time, that it was probably one less chance of their secret ever getting out and said nothing. Now, realising that it was not the correct person that was dead he wanted assurance from Kevin that their relationship had not been compromised. Kevin, still in the depts of despair since realising he had killed the wrong woman, could not take any more and in a fit of rage strangled Colm.

    A month later a report, following an investigation in Holland, into a murder in Spain, was highlighted in every newspaper throughout Europe giving the details of a tragic story. The sad life of a mentally disturbed woman and how she had conceived a murder was graphically revealed. She had been stopped and searched as she landed, at Schiphol airport, in Amsterdam coming off a flight from Ireland by an officer who thought the briefcase she was carrying looked like the one he was watching out for in connection with a diamond investigation. The briefcase contained over forty thousand US dollars for which she had no explanation. It was learned that early in her life she was involved in the cover up of the death of her brother which haunted her to the point of distraction and she was in and out of mental institutions for many years as she tried to overcome her instability. During the course of her treatment she had met another patient of similar height and age but more importantly with the same name and an evil plan festered in her troubled mind. Although she had many breakdowns, when she was lucid, she was involved in a world of crime. She was a seasoned diamond thief with the thoughts of making one big final heist after which she could retire and enjoy the fruits of her labour. Her new found double gave her all types of options as long as she could be creative and duplicate a large birthmark on her face. That they looked so alike and both lived on the edge of reality was uncanny but she planned to put it to her advantage. Setting her up, by allowing her to live in her house, she waited patiently for an opportunity to present itself and knew that she could call on her to, unknowingly, help her. Hearing of a diamond transaction where a large sum of money would be exchanged she thought how much easier it would be to just get her hands on the cash. Her contacts told her of the Spanish hotel in Bilbao where the thief was staying and not realising that it was one of her ex-army comrades she began to formulate her plans. She provided herself with the perfect alibi when, after using an indelible type of makeup, she painted a purplish copy of her birthmark on Lena's face and sent her on an errand to Ireland. She only needed it to last a few days to convince those who saw her to believe it was her. She never meant for her to die and expected her to be home shortly after she had got the cash. She arrived at the hotel as Gareth was leaving and followed him to Madrid where she killed him and took the cash. Later when she heard that her alibi had been killed before she had committed her murder she decided to travel to Ireland where she went to the B&B and removed any evidence that her double had left behind. She never went to court as she was judged mentally unfit to stand trial and was placed in a mental institution. Lena Nowak was the third person who thought they could live on the proceeds of that sale of diamonds and she like Gareth and Luke, ended up without anything.

What a tragic ending for a group of army comrades. Ten years of unhappiness worrying about an accident that could have been reported without recrimination. Three unnecessary deaths from within the group and an unfortunate woman murdered just by having a similar name. One person charged with two of the murders and another, due to her mental instability, unable to answer for committing her murder. Although not directly connected to any of the murders a person badly injured possibly without part of his memory for ever. The final three carrying their guilt for the rest of their lives.

Ingram Content Group UK Ltd.
Milton Keynes UK
UKHW011357050623
422897UK00004B/357